CN00842524

Also by Michael Bailey

Novels

Palindrome Hannah

Phoenix Rose

Psychotropic Dragon

Novellas

Agatha's Barn
(a Carpenter's Farm story)

Novelettes

Our Children, Our Teachers

Collections

Scales and Petals

Inkblots and Blood Spots

Oversight

Edited by Michael Bailey

Anthologies

Pellucid Lunacy

Chiral Mad

Chiral Mad 2

Qualia Nous

The Library of the Dead

Chiral Mad 3

You, Human

Adam's Ladder
(with Darren Speegle)

Chiral Mad 4: An Anthology of Collaborations
(with Lucy A. Snyder)

Miscreations: Gods, Monstrosities & Other Horrors
(with Doug Murano)

Prisms
(with Darren Speegle)

the impossible weight of life

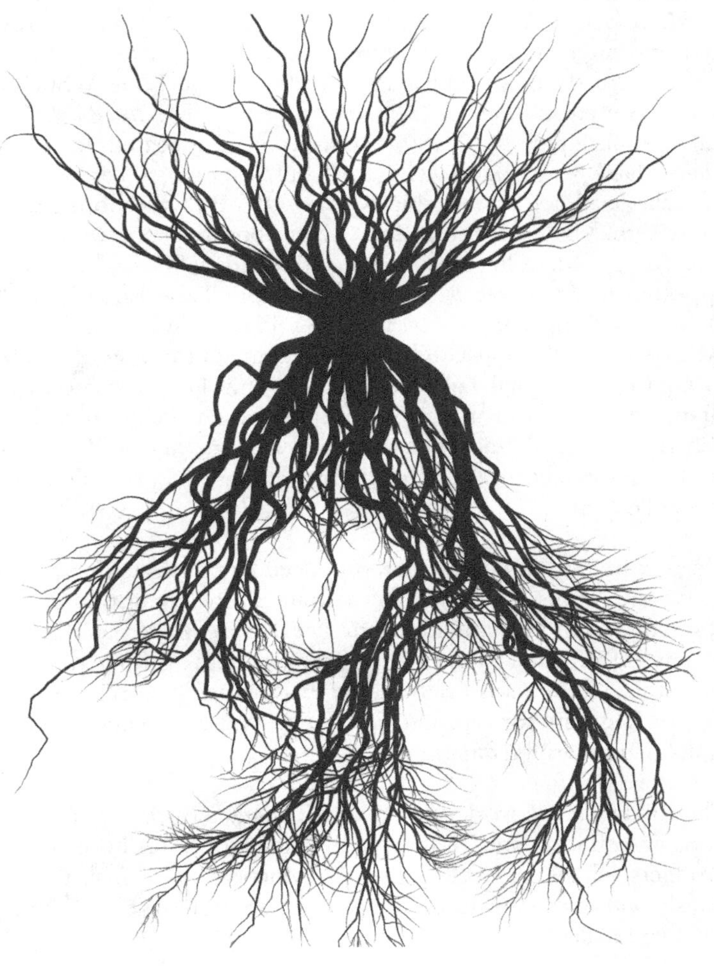

fiction and poetry by michael bailey

Cover and interior design by Michael Bailey

"Time is a Face on the Water" first appeared in *Borderlands 6* (Borderlands Press), © 2016, nominated for the Bram Stoker Awards ® for Superior Achievement in Short Fiction; "Speaking Cursive" first appeared in *Birthing Monsters: Frankenstein's Cabinet of Curiosities and Cruelties* (Firbolg Publishing), © 2018; "The Long White Line" first appeared in *Lost Highways: Dark Fictions from the Road* (Crystal Lake Publishing), © 2018; "Möbius" first appeared in *The Pulp Horror Book of Phobias, Vol. 2* (LVP Publications), © 2020; "Ghosts of Calistoga" first appeared in *Reflections* (LVP Publications), © 2020; "The Other Side of Semicolons" first appeared in *Monsters of Any Kind* (Independent Legions Publishing), © 2018; "Essential Oils" first appeared in *18 Wheels of Science Fiction* (Big Time Books), © 2018; "Gave" first appeared in *After Sundown* (Flametree Press), © 2020; "I Will Be the Reflection Until the End" first appeared in *Tales from the Lake, Vol. 4* (Crystal Lake Publishing), © 2017, nominated for the Bram Stoker Awards ® for Superior Achievement in Short Fiction; "Shades of Red" first appeared in *Poetry Showcase, Vol. 6* (Horror Writers Association), © 2019; all other stories and poems are new to this collection.

Published by Written Backwards
www.nettirw.com

ISBN: 978-1-7355981-1-6 / Hardback Edition
ISBN: 978-1-7355981-0-9 / Paperback Edition

for Terica

the impossible weight of life

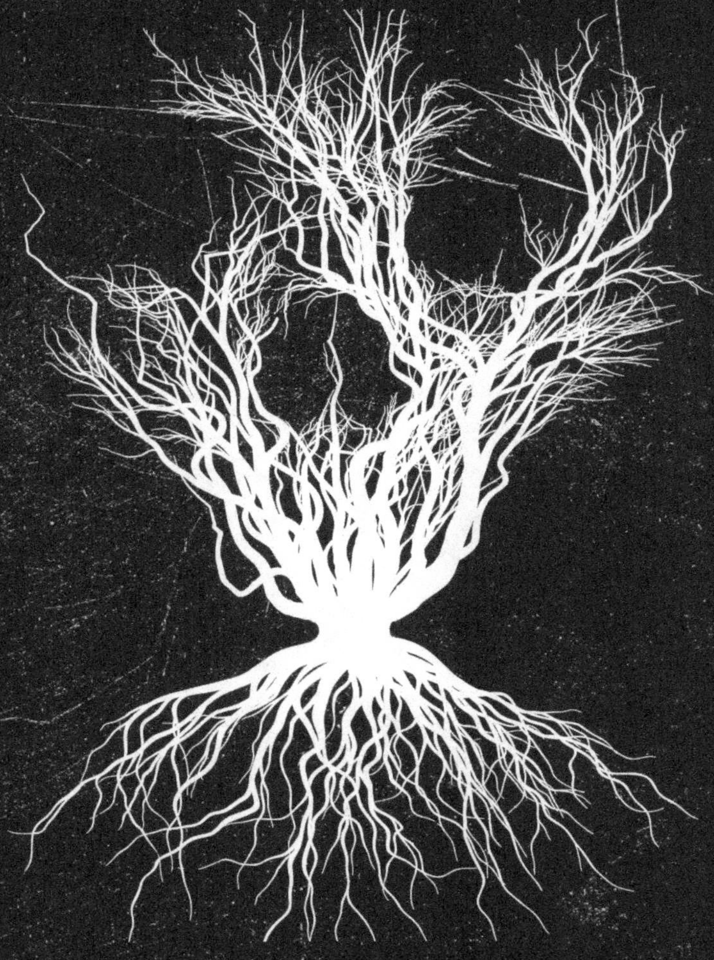

stories

poems

loosed earth

A burning world
prays yearning for rain
during a pained draught
no doubt which comes
too late for some
to extinguish last hotspots
brought upon past soft plots
sending a simmering ground
glimmering with ash-mud
to slip-slide the sides
in scare-rides
not meant for women
nor men or children

caught mixed in the crud
in fraught games of chance
to play in avalanches of unstable
rubble unable to cling to root
and soot attempting to
hold a cold and crumbling
foundation together
and will this never end
or go on forever
as the terrible
treble-tremble sings
a sad ensemble
of oversaturated help

to sated gods
devoid of love
bringing new horrors
for hours or forever
as those coerced
to flee are freed
then forced to plea
on frayed knees
praying for heat
in dry pouts
as they cry out
for fires
to mask the floods

time is a face on the water

Act 1: The Past

What kind of play is this?

Günay admired the rivulets interrupting the otherwise placid pool of water in the creek out back, the place he went to think, to reflect on life and what it all meant.

Death had taken his daughter, Airavata. He and Luci chose the name after looking through a book on names and originations. Airavata, sometimes Air for short, meant 'child of water,' which they thought clever since Gün's own name was Turkish for *sun* and Luci derived from the Latin *lux*, meaning *light*. From sun and light they had created a daughter they had sometimes called *air* and sometimes called *water*, and she was gone. Ten years ago she'd died. Like it was yesterday.

A tragedy?

Yes, life's often a tragedy, but sometimes much more …

A comedy?

No, no one's laughing.

A history?

Yes, there's much history involved.

Life was a beautiful play, for the most part, full of rich colors, warmth, love, and characters, *so* many characters, full of dialogue—sometimes internal, but more often spoken aloud whether necessary or not—and of course life was full of memorable scenes, one after another after another, like rivulets of water dancing chaotically together; and yet, sometimes life quieted down and turned placid, allowing you to reflect more clearly on the three acts of *past*, *present* and *future*.

Act 1, in Gün's case, encompassed approximately thirty years of his life, and could be summarized by the following: birth, childhood, adolescence, transition to adulthood, sexuality, self-discovery, finding and marrying the light of his life known as Luci, and then writing the first act of Airavata's play, which, since life turns like a wheel, included her birth, childhood, adolescence ....

Airavata had lived a one-act play.

And now I'm entering Act 2 of my own two- or, if I'm lucky, three-act play, Gün mused, staring at the water.

The creek, like the rest of the state, had mostly dried up. Sparse rain the night before trickled water down the creek, which travelled the long path from the mountain and eventually through their backyard. Such a wonderful sound. Small pools of black had welled where it could as insects skimmed over the surface; green mossy river rocks below created the dark appearance. The rain often summoned newts and less-often salamanders to the uncovered rocks, and Gün noticed now an orange-bellied creature with bubbly brown skin surfacing for air.

He and Air had often carried these timid California newts around the property, and they didn't seem to mind; they held on tight, in fact, with a strong embrace, as if affectionate. The *Taricha torosa*, he'd later discovered, secreted a potent neurotoxin called tetrodotoxin, hundreds of times more toxic than cyanide, the same toxin found in pufferfish and certain frogs.

They're not dangerous by any means, Gün assured Luci on more than one occasion. *Well, they are, but only if you poke them with a stick real hard, and only if you ingest what they excrete.*

It was a chain reaction of events, much like life, that made the California newt so interesting. To protect itself from birds, snakes, and other prey, the seemingly innocent creature had evolved over time to excrete the deadly toxin, arching its back and writhing to expose the bright orange warning color of its belly if pierced, making the newt nearly untouchable as a species. Yet, as if a longwinded Darwinian joke, a few species of Garter snake evolved as well, developing a genetic resistance to tetrodotoxin, putting this particular animal back in the food chain. And now they were nearly extinct.

But who the hell cares about newts, Gün thought.

As if in response, the newt crawled ever so slowly onto a dry rock and studied him.

A blue and white sky reflected against the black-mirror surface of the small pool, as well as the autumnal-changing yellows, browns and reds of grapevines intertwined in the branches of the trees lining the creek bed. Seafoam green Spanish moss draped over limbs like delicate lace. Rainbow colors surrounded him as sunlight permeated the canopy in stripes.

Lux, he thought. *Luci. My light.*

When placed together, their names formed a compound word: *sunlight.*

Look, a heart, Air had said one day, holding a large crimson grape leaf against her chest. Gün took in the memory, as well as the crisp smell of redwoods and birches and dying grapes as the wind offered all of it to him. They had sometimes floated leaves down the creek when it was running well to see whose would reach the waterfall by the big rock the fastest.

Gün found a yellow grape leaf and placed it in the water. It floated alone, not moving anywhere, but spinning in slow circles because there was not enough current.

Luci took Airavata's death the hardest. She rarely spoke, burying herself in cleaning and other such chores whether necessary or not, and she refused to touch Air's room, as if waiting for her to return one day. It took her and Gün three days to talk about what had happened, and even after they talked about it, neither had anything much to say. This lack of communication nearly wrecked their marriage, but they'd somehow stuck together and survived the roughest of times. It wasn't Luci's fault, but *both* their faults. Communication's a collaborative enterprise.

Will she stay? Gün asked the water, meaning Luci, meaning would she stay alongside him to see how their play would ultimately end, to see what kind of a play they had lived.

He looked at his reflection.

His reflection looked back.

Ten years, he thought. *Will she stay for ten more years?*

Water rippled from the wind, from the bugs, from floating hearts and other debris, from the deadly newt crawling back under the surface. Ravens fluttered and cawed from the treetops, as if laughing from above at his internal dialogue. The scent of leaves decomposing on the wet ground at the edge of the creek was aromatic, along with the mushrooms and lichen growing on fallen branches and the snapped fir tree dangling perpendicular over the water.

Then the face changed, quicker than the season.

His once brown hair a little less brown, with perhaps peppered gray, perhaps thinner; his facial hair lighter as well, his cheeks more gaunt, his eyes a shade darker and baggier.

He was older.

Ten years. This is what I will look like in ten years.

A hazy version of Luci's face peered over his reflection's shoulder, like a heat wave over hot asphalt. She, too, appeared ten years older. Crow's feet had begun at the corners of her eyes, her face thinner, her expression sad.

This is what she will look like in ten years.

She was a stunning woman, always. Add another ten years, and another ten years, and, hell, even another, and she'd still be as beautiful as the day he fell in love with her all those years ago. But that was more of the past. Love's a hard thing to find after tragedy.

Gün turned and was surprised to find Luci standing there. This was his daydream, after all, *his* glimpse into the looking glass. She didn't say anything at first, only put a hand on his shoulder. He put his hand over hers and together they looked at the creek.

The high afternoon sun had dropped closer to the horizon to become a setting sun, the colors changing once more before their final fade to colorless night; the yellows more orange, the oranges more red, and the reds becoming various shades of purple like the mountain range to the east. The colors seemed warmer, almost glowing, although it was much colder than when he had first come out to the creek to think.

"I found something new," she said, meaning something of Airavata's.

Ten years had passed and they were still finding pieces of her past scattered around them.

A week after her funeral, which was also a week after Air's tenth birthday, Gün found a shriveled balloon left over from her birthday party. He found it in the laundry hamper, of all places, and at first thought it was a bunched-up sock mixed in with the rest of her dirty clothes. Air had often worn bright socks, not necessarily matching. And he remembered knowing then that Luci would wash these clothes, even though she'd never be able to wear them again. It was a red oxidized balloon that he found, like a blotch of memory, with some of Air's breath trapped inside.

He'd held the balloon close to his chest, sobbing tearlessly, chest caving painfully with each uncontrollable spasm. *Some-*

times it hurts to cry, his mother once told him, and it was then he finally understood her meaning. The tears eventually came, and they did hurt, and by that time Luci had come looking for him because he'd been gone for so long.

"I said I found something new," she said.

"Yeah?"

"Where were you just now?"

"I was just remembering the balloon."

She squeezed his hand tighter and he squeezed back, three times.

I love you, it meant; one squeeze for each word.

Some words were harder to say after losing a daughter, but some words could be said without talking at all.

She squeezed back, two times, ever so softly.

I know.

Airavata had created the secret language, perhaps a dozen or so phrases through various hand squeezes. It was one of the few of things of hers that didn't hurt to keep.

They held onto the balloon a few more days after finding it, and it sometimes joined them at the dinner table, or on the dash of the car when they went out for a drive, and every day the balloon shrank, and what was left of Air inside slowly dwindled, and dwindled ....

"Yeah?" she said.

"I remember the smell," he said. "We were so afraid of losing her, you know? Her breath was in there, that small part of her we could keep, but by holding onto the balloon and not releasing her breath meant we could lose her forever, even though by cutting open the balloon we'd get her for that brief moment, and still lose her forever."

She squeezed his hand, once, for a long time. It didn't mean anything specific, but somehow meant something that couldn't be expressed in words, and they both understood.

Luci had squeezed his hand like that the moment before they cut open the balloon to let the last of Air go.

"It smelled like huckleberry lip gloss," she said.

"It did."

Gün smiled, and although he couldn't see Luci's smile, he knew it was there.

Luci pointed over his shoulder to another dry rock.

The orange-bellied newt had returned, or maybe one of his friends.

"She used to love carrying those around," she said. "Remember the second year we lived here, she found five of them, or six, and she came running to the back patio holding all of them at once?"

"And the next day she found ten."

Another long squeeze, which didn't mean anything, but meant the world to him.

"What did you find?"

"The music box," she said, and he understood her melancholy.

They had kept Air's baby teeth in a cheap music box Luci found one weekend while thrifting. The box was wooden, covered with intricate carvings of flowers. When you opened the lid it smelled like cedar, and what was left of the ballerina inside—just her feet and ankles since the rest of her had broken off long ago—spun round while the tune of "Swan Lake" played on what sounded like the world's smallest xylophone.

"I forgot all about the music box," she said. I was dusting the dresser in our room and moved a pile of books out of the way and knocked it to the floor. The lid won't close so the music kept playing and playing, so I spun the shoes by hand until the music stopped. It was an awful sound, like a mechanical grinding. I think I broke it for good. And then I saw her teeth, Air's teeth, scattered on the carpet. I found them all. I counted. Some with dried blood, and—"

"Luci," he said, and glanced over his shoulder.

It was the first time they'd looked into each other's eyes since the reflection in the water of the creek, but that wasn't really looking; that had been a cheat.

She had aged ten years.

She's been crying, he told himself. *She's been crying and her eyes are puffy and dark—no, no, she can't be older—and her eyes are tired, like mine, that's all.*

Luci always had dirty-blonde hair, but it seemed dirtier now, and longer. Her hand, still in his, felt lighter, her skin more delicate, papery. She had definitely aged.

And his own weathered hand—

"I just wanted to tell you so you wouldn't be upset," she said.

"We'll find a new music box."

Gün squeezed her hand, three times.

I love you.

The secret message went unanswered as Luci slid her hand free. She offered an expressionless flat smile, turned away, and headed back to the house.

Act 2: The Present

You'll find love when you stop looking for it. This was another of his mother's sayings, and for most of his life, Gün thought she had been full of shit. Many years before crashing into Luci, he had dated, looking for his match, the perfect woman—woman after woman—and at first he thought he found the right one and married his mistake, then divorced, and almost married again. He had eventually given up on women at the age of thirty, telling his friends he was happy alone, better off alone, in fact, that he was *happier*, that if he had to live alone for the rest of his life, so be it. He was good with that.

Gün had stopped looking for love, and that's precisely the moment he found love, without looking at all. His mother had been right all those years.

Luci found *him*, in other words. They fell in love, stayed in love, made love, and together created a beautiful child. Happily ever after, or so they thought.

Gün found himself at the end of Act 1, *the past*, and the end of an agonizing transition to Act 2, *the present*. Life, the unforgiving wheel, turned every once in a while, making everything look all so familiar once again ....

You'll find love when you stop looking for it.

True then. True now.

Airavata haunted their lives whenever they stopped looking for her, it seemed. Scattered pieces from her past kept cropping up in the strangest of places. It was a different kind of love, but still love. Sometimes the haunts were good, but more often they were bad.

This went on for another nine years; their daughter now gone for twenty.

After much counseling, they decided to throw it all away. Everything. And it was about damn time. *Holding onto the past only brings heartache*, they were told by some shrink. *It's unhealthy*. Airavata was gone, but as long as her *things* were still around, her absence would continue their assault on their emotions, and would ultimately destroy them.

That's all they really were, just *things*; the memories of Airavata mattered, not her personal belongings. They got rid of it all, donating her life possessions to thrift stores and charitable organizations, where they would never have to see them again, and it was hard, so very hard. But sometimes these material things resurfaced when they least expected, like the teeth in the music box, or the mood ring Gün now held in his hand.

Her bed—not slept in for twenty years—was the last of her things to go, or so they thought, their neighbors next door finally taking it off their hands. Gün found the cheap silver ring smashed into the carpet beneath one of the drawers built into the bedframe. He slid the ring next to his wedding band and within seconds the plastic disc or stone or whatever was set in the center turned a light green color, whatever that meant. When he removed the ring, it left behind a similar color on his finger. Air had worn the cheap ring—a keepsake from some game at one of her friend's birthday parties—until the day she'd lost it.

Gün knew why rings turned fingers green, but that's not what bothered him now. What bothered him was the fact that his finger was green. He hadn't worn it long enough for the chemical reaction to take place between the acids on his skin and the metal of the ring, which meant Air's skin had caused the reaction however many years prior, and he had transferred a part of his dead daughter's past onto his finger.

He tossed the ring into the trash container next to the toilet in the bathroom and made his way to the sink to wash off the green, but it wouldn't come off with water. The soap dispenser was also out, so of course he checked under the sink, where he found Airavata's pink hairbrush hiding among the toiletries, with some of her hair caught in the bristles—his dead daughter's hair. He brought the brush to his nose, but the scent of her strawberry blonde hair was long gone. It smelled like the pipes under the sink. He tossed the hairbrush into the trash and missed and—

"I found her phone," Luci said from the other room, "my old one we gave her when she was six and wanted to have a phone like mom. Remember?"

"I do. Luci, we need to—"

"She used to record herself singing."

"The Redolent. She loved a band called The Redolent for some reason."

"I followed bands like that, too, when I was her age. I've been charging the phone. Want to listen?"

Gün released a held breath he was saving to tell her *no.*

"It's not a *thing*; it's a memory," she said, and that seemed to make sense, because memories were not meant to be thrown away.

Without saying anything, they had agreed to listen.

The rain won't fall on the both of us
If I pull you in close
And you pull me in close
The sky, although it cries
The sky won't cry on the both of us

Her voice, like a tone-deaf angel, ripped open his heart and flooded him with warmth, catching him off-guard because hearing her voice after all these years was something he had not prepared for, and it was … It was "Though It Rains." She had always skipped the second stanza because she could never quite remember the lines, and so she'd burst right into part of the chorus, nearly yelling—

And the water cascades
Cascades, cascades, cascades …

—and more often than not he and Luci would sing along at this point. Luci was in fact mouthing the words now, singing along with their dead daughter, tears streaming down her face, fucking up the lyrics like always, skipping verses:

The rain, yes, it will fall
If you're the one I choose
And I'm the one you choose
The sky, yes, it will cry
But it won't cry on the both of us

And when the chorus repeated, now both Luci and Gün sang with their daughter, who was anything but dead in their hearts, although their broken voices were just above a whisper: "*Cascades, cascades, cascades …*"

The pink hairbrush finally found its way into the trash, along with some strands of hair, but Gün rescued the mood ring from the wads of tissues and cotton swabs. He didn't tell Luci he still had it—secretly transferring the thing from pants pocket to pants pocket over the last three days, sometimes reaching in to feel the cold, sometimes slipping a finger through the band and wondering what color it turned within the darkness.

He eventually brought it with him to the creek, where he could hide it from Luci forever. It had rained hard, so the creek had transformed from trickling to flowing, how he remembered it the springs and summers when the three of them would walk the creek in their rain boots.

He slid the ring onto his finger one last time and spun it around and around, making sure it left a ghostly ring of green behind, and smiled when the plastic or stone or whatever it was in the middle turned dark blue, which he remembered meant either *calm* or *happy*, and then tossed it into the largest pool of water. The blackness of the creek swallowed the ring, but he'd for now on know it was there, hidden below the surface, where it would forever remain colorless.

Gün didn't like keeping secrets like this from Luci, but was sure Luci had kept or had hidden certain things without him knowing. Some secrets were good secrets after all.

He and Luci had gotten better over the last ten years. Getting rid of Airavata's *things* had helped, yet a small part of him wondered if the happiness would last, whether or not they would ever return to normalcy, whether or not they could ever love each other the way they had before—

When was the last time either had ever spoken those magical three words: *I love you?* Their hands had symbolically said those *un*-words a number of times, along with other *un*-spoken phrases in their secret language, but when was the last time they were spoken aloud?

Twenty years.

Jesus.

Gün crouched down and leaned over the water, once again looking at his reflection. He remembered the last time he'd visited the creek, over ten years ago, and had asked the all-important question: *Will she stay?*

The answer had been yes, and she had stayed.

But for how much longer?

Will she stay? he had asked the water again. *Will she stay for ten more years?*

They hadn't aged ten years the moment he peered into their future all those years ago; they had *lived* those years, together. Hadn't they? The last ten years were a blur. Had they really lived *ten* additional years together in such unhappiness, and holding onto Air's things for so long? Had it taken them *twenty* fucking years to finally rid their lives of her personal belongings, to try to forget her? No, that wasn't right. They would always remember her.

Time is a wheel, he mused, *sometimes turning slowly, sometimes spinning out of control.*

Time had spun for the last ten years, and had for some reason stopped at this exact moment, on this cold winter morning, so he could once again reflect on life.

The wonderful colors of autumn were gone, the leaves fallen, the world moodless.

Although the creek flowed steadily along, the pool of water over which he leaned was placid as could be, the insects gone, the newts and salamanders hibernated, or whatever they did in the winter, the birds long-migrated to warmer, more lively places, and the life around him, for the most part, silent; only the soft, therapeutic sounds of water and wind kept him company.

Two heart-shaped leaves slow-raced along the surface and fell over the waterfall by the large rock; neither won, but tied as they tumbled over.

Will she stay? Gün once again asked the water, meaning Luci. And he wondered for how long. *Will she stay for ten more years?*

Will we ever get over our loss? Will we last?

A brown redwood leaf with spiky needles fell from above just then, landing on the face of his reflection, rippling the water, changing him, aging him.

When the obsidian water once again settled to mirror glass, Gün's beard and sideburns had become half brown, half gray, along with the rest of the hair on his head, which appeared sparse in places, wispier, his hairline higher. His nose and ears had stretched a fraction longer, it seemed, his eyes swallowed by dark, tired circles, the color in his eyes milkier. His reflection had aged ten years, not only physically but emotionally. Gün touched his face and watched his reflection do the same; both sets of hands felt weathered skin, and—

He waited for Luci to join him in the water.

Will she stay for ten more years?

And he waited, and waited, his reflection transforming.

His heart sank and felt heavy, although he knew this was all in his head. He hadn't aged ten more years, or twenty, since he had asked the question again. It was the water creating the wrinkles, not time; the wheel could not be forced to turn.

Will she stay for ten more years?

"*Cascades, cascades, cascades …*" he sang.

He felt thirty years older now, could feel the change in the cold aches of his bones, in the more difficult way he breathed, and by his reflection becoming out-of-focus.

"Will she stay?" he said aloud. "Will Luci stay with me ten more years?"

Gün cried again, the image in the reflection blurring.

Will she stay just ten more years?

And blurring.

He was losing it, fucking *losing* it, having a panic attack, which he'd had once before when finding the red balloon with the last of Air trapped inside, and that's exactly how he felt now, his air trapped inside an ever-shriveling balloon and unable to escape, his chest tightening, his heart palpitating ....

A murder of crows—what he had read once were the harbingers of death—cackled above, hidden in the trees and inviting Death to take him away, to be with Airavata—

And then she came.

Gün could barely see her through the tears, and the *blur*, but she was there.

A reflection of Luci stood over the reflection of his shoulder.

She put a papery-bony hand onto his shoulder and his heart could once again beat, his lungs could once again breathe.

He put his own aged hand over hers and squeezed one long time, which didn't mean anything, but meant everything, and she squeezed back, three times.

"I will stay with you until the end," she said; and had.

He could never ask Luci to do something so difficult, but she had stayed.

Gün wiped at the tears with his free hand, and their reflection came into better focus, although the phantasm of their potential future remained blurry as hell.

"*If you're the one I choose*," she sang, "*and I'm the one you choose.*"

Together they sang the chorus.

He didn't turn around, couldn't look her in the face just yet, and that was okay. It would all be okay. Instead, he squeezed her hand in a way he knew would make her smile.

Luci reached a hand across his shoulder, not pointing at a newt this time, but holding a pair of glasses, which he instantly knew were *his* glasses, although he couldn't—but at the same time *could*—remember wearing glasses and, still holding her hand, took them with his other and shook them open, placing them onto his face the way he had done either a million times before or had never at all.

The world came into focus.

Gün looked at their reflection in the water, and then turned to face Luci.

They were so very old.

He squeezed her hand, three times, the way Airavata had taught them.

She squeezed back, three times, and said the words.

He said them too.

What kind of play is this? he wondered, but he already knew. Their life had not been a single type of Shakespearian play, but a combination of all three: *a tragedy*, *a history*, *a comedy*. But would they ever laugh again?

They both returned their attention to the water, and perhaps asked the same questions to the looking glass:

Can we ever have her back? Can we have her back for just ten more years?

Act 3: The Future

Sometimes the last act of a play can be short, and sweet; sometimes those are the best kinds of plays, or so Günay believed, for he and Luci had seen many over the years.

Their daughter was turning ten and she wanted red balloons.

"What do you want to do after the party?" Luci asked her.

Air filled the first of what would be ten balloons, one for each of her years, which had become the tradition over the years, something she had wanted; next year she'd have eleven, and then twelve, and so on.

"When I'm as old as you," she said, meaning her father, "I *may* need some help."

And they laughed.

She caught her breath, tied off the last of the balloons, and flicked it across the room.

Airavata held her mother's cell phone, the old one they gave her when she was six and wanted to have a phone like mom so she could record videos of her singing The Redolent. Her voice, that tone-deaf angel, ripped open his heart once again and flooded him with warmth as she remembered a stanza from "Though It Rains" that she sometimes forgot:

The sky won't cry on the both of us
When I pull you in close
And you pull me in close
The rain, although it falls
The rain won't fall on the both of us

Luci sang along for the chorus, and Gün joined in, the three of them bursting right through the chorus, their voices cracking, nearly yelling, and finally breaking into another fit of laughter.

What kind of play is this?

hurt people hurt people

Tears are the means of editing the self
so why the need to ~~improve~~ revise?
The poison-pen mouth
breaks open
seeps
forever-stains
each ~~soul~~ page spot-tinged
    / soaking the book of life

What's the purpose
of hurt people hurting people?
The face of fear
falls apart
disintegrates
never remains
once ~~un~~truths are revealed
/ covering the floor with dust

~~There's not enough torment inside the self~~
~~There's too much torment inside the self~~
There's ~~too much~~ enough ~~too much~~ torment inside the self
so why the need to redirect?
The horror-stricken mask
splits wide
cracks
ever-broken
        / ending the ~~dream~~ nightmare

speaking cursive

We vacuumed her face; our fondest memory of mom before the alcohol drank her.

High school had been a blur, all four years. We rode the bus while freshmen and sophomores, and then—in the summer we changed from brother / sister to something more like friends—we pooled our money working car washes and other odd jobs to buy a piece-of-crap Honda Civic so we could drive ourselves out of the mud. That's when mom slid most, when we stopped *needing* her, when she started slugging straight from the bottle.

She'd given birth to us, sure, but the stuff she drank impregnated her belly with a new kind of monstrosity, something black and parasitic and ever-controlling. And it always wanted so badly out of her, like the rain out of the clouds that night.

"*You think I'note know what're doing can—*" she said over a crash of thunder.

Speaking cursive, we called it, when her words slurred.

Dad couldn't stand being with her, couldn't raise us on his own, so he did the only thing he did well: he left.

"Your mother and I," he'd said, his sentences like his drink—always started but never finished—"We think it's best that I …" and "The two of you will be …" and other such fragments of failed parenting. He'd tried keeping up with her for a while, with the drink, but unlike mom, his glass was always half-empty and hers half-full. Did this make him a pessimist? If so, what did that make *her?* Sometimes he'd pour a finger of whiskey or scotch or bourbon, and he'd swirl it, if only to stare at it for a while, to have something in common with her, but eventually there was only one glass leaving rings on the coffee table in the living room.

"Shit," one of us had said, the plastic bag of little white beads exploding.

We were filling beanbags, which mom thought would be easier than buying new ones, or cheaper. Instead of the bag tearing at the perforated top it blew out from the bottom and for a moment of slowed time the room became a snow globe. Styrofoam fell over us, onto the couch, the carpet, mostly onto mom, some cascading down her arm and pouring into her glass.

You are my sunshine when I am the rain.

On the counter, the Morton salt container sat forgotten after unfinished TV dinners. The girl in a rain slicker holding an umbrella offered us a fortune: *When it rains it pours.*

Why did we both look first to *her*—to the yellow-jacket girl, not mom—as staticy white balls blanketed our creator? The beads stuck to mom's hair and shoulders like dandruff, and when she breathed in some of the beads sucked into her mouth and up her nose and back out again in a strange cycle. She coughed, once, but slept through the event, sawing logs like she always had when passed out on the couch.

She took the brunt of the mess, and we laughed at the sight of her as rain beat hard against the window. We didn't stop laughing until the rain outside turned to hail, the sky yelling at us to stop, perhaps. Storms: both inside and outside the house.

When it rains it pours.

White stuck to us as well. A real mess.

Mom had this zigzag scar connecting her left ear to the side of her head, like something out of a bad horror movie. We were both afraid of the off-colored skin there, as if touching the pink would spread it to our fingers or other places. The scar was something evil, we knew, because hair never grew there. She'd told us once that when she was in her teens she'd been in a horrible car accident, and glass from the driver's side window had sheared off that ear completely, and so doctor's had reattached it. *Never looked the same after the surgery*, she'd told us. And for some reason, we were always afraid that if we startled her awake, she might tear it back off with those after-waking hands of hers; they'd sometimes claw the air.

"Mom?" one of us called, trying the impossible task of waking *her* but not the sleeping demon. "Mom!" one of us said, loud as a car crash.

We patted her on the shoulder, the three of us looking ridiculous. Those were good smiles, good laughs.

The monster stirred, slurred, said something incomprehensible like "*Constan-sloping*" in her sleep, and then snored with old-alcohol stench, like some stranger's backwash left in a beer bottle overnight. Mom sat mostly upright on the couch: a drunken-posed manikin. The white beads statically-clung to the throw-blanket covering her upper half, her lower half hanging over the edge of the couch, with one of her legs on the coffee table and the other on the ground. The television, on but muted, displayed white static from a non-channel, as if mimicking us.

"Mom?"

Nothing but rhythmic sawing.

Together we make a rainbow, like a smile upside-down.

We stood behind her, looking over mom's horrid upside-down-face. The smile was a lie, we knew, a frown from a different perspective. One of her eye sockets was completely filled in with the little white fluffs—a Styrofoam patch—and her mouth open wide, the beads like broken teeth. She nearly gargled them.

We lifted her foot a few inches above the coffee table and dropped it, because sometimes the noise would wake her and we'd done it before. Her foot fell like a thunderclap, but she slept through the ordeal, like she'd sometimes sleep through *everything.* One of us lifted the foot higher, five or so inches, dropped it. *Bang!* A flash of light outside. The foot was lifted even higher, enough to hurt. *Bang!* Another flash of light, brighter. We dropped her foot three times, filling the room with thunder.

Nothing.

She slept like the dead.

We'd found the note dad left behind for mom. His scribble-like handwriting was at least legible, but progressively worsened as his final unfinished words to mom came to a close. He'd cried, we knew, because of the round splotches that had fallen and dried upon the page.

> *I'm not sure when we fell apart, or if there ever came a defining moment, but here we are. I am who I've become. You are who you've become. If we've become anything together these last twenty years, we've become incompatible. Broken. I can't do this anymore … Our children need us now more than ever, but I—*

That's where the note ended, and she'd never had a chance to read it. We crumpled the note, uncrumpled it, read it again, and ultimately burned dad's words with a match over the sink after making a pact never to tell her we found it. He'd be back, we knew. Dad would be back, because he'd tried to leave once before. He'd left and had come back, and we couldn't let him hurt mom that way, not again.

She hadn't noticed his absence the first few days.

"Have you seen your father?" she asked one morning while sober, and we both shook our heads, both thought of the note and looked to each other for support.

Mom let it go and made our lunches, as she had every day before the bus picked us up for school. With a Sharpie she'd write notes on Post-Its, put them in our lunches, and leave them for us to find—to later remember, like the slogan on the salt container—these short mom-isms in script-like handwriting that bled through:

Love you, sweetie! or a heart drawn around the word *ALWAYS*, or *Hope you like the chocolate!*

She'd sometimes leave squares of Ghirardelli or Dove dark chocolates, bite-sized Snickers or Twix. She'd always put something fun in our lunches, and every time the lunch bell rang it was something to look forward to, like pieces of the mom we wanted to remember. The notes reminded us that she was still inside the evil creature she'd become after the sun fell below the horizon, before she'd drink herself into the dark.

Even with dad gone, living with mom felt like living with two people.

We can change, or we can be the change.

Sometimes she'd leave good mom-isms like that. And sometimes she'd forget. Sometimes we'd come home from school and she'd be waiting for us at the door, drink already in hand—*her fourth, her fifth?*—and she'd smile through whatever happy-mask face she conjured, but even children notice when a smile is forced; children notice the red left behind in eyes after a good cry. And we'd smile forced smiles of our own, and tell her about our day.

Her sixth, her seventh?

"Your father'sis not—" she tried telling us one night, when she finally realized dad was not gone, but *gone*. She'd finished her drink—the recipes becoming less and less important—and ice clinked in the silence that followed.

She cried into her glass that night, simply *looking* at us, *through* us, brought the glass to her lips and drank her tears. Sometimes she'd rub the scar.

"He'll be back," one of us said, and that was enough to get through the night.

If we've become anything together over these last twenty years, we've become incompatible. Broken. I can't do this anymore.

Love is like this chocolate.

Inside a dark chocolate Dove wrapper—accompanying one of mom's notes—were words printed on the foil by the manufacturer, a fortune left behind from the devoured square of chocolate, perhaps:

I may be gone, but there are others …

When the vacuum hummed to life, not even *that* was enough to wake her. We took turns cleaning the beanbag snow. Each bead held an idiosyncratic-static charge, sticking to *everything*, to us, the vacuum slurping them up with crackly pops but also moving them around the room, creating even *more* static. They were everywhere. Complete and utter chaos. The clean-up was as easy as pushing chains up a sand dune.

We managed to get about half the beads into the beanbags before zipping them shut, scooping handfuls upon handfuls—both cleaning and spreading the mess—but the other half littered the living room. Mom continued breathing them, perhaps ingesting a few. And every time we brushed beads off her body we thought doing so might wake her, afraid of letting out what riled inside. But she was *out*, and so the creature stayed in her belly. Whenever she got *this* bad, nothing could wake her. If she stirred, she'd speak cursive and nothing more.

We were safe, we knew.

The hose attachment seemed to work best, and we used it to suck up the beads that made their way under the couch and into the various crevices, and then one of us looked to the other, to mom. Then our eyes met again, and it was understood what needed to be done.

I love you both, so much.

I love you both, so much.

We always compared the notes mom left us in our lunches because they were always different, until they *stopped* being different, which happened more often after dad left. Sometimes her handwritten notes would repeat, sometimes the words would be as indecipherable as her slurs, and sometimes one of us would find a reused note in one of our lunch pails. And sometimes she'd forget to write anything at all.

Together we make a rainbow, like a smile upside-down.

WHERE IS YOUR FATHER?!

[a blank pink Post-It]

We vacuumed the beads, even those covering mom. The impossibly-loud noise never once woke her, although she swatted the nozzle on occasion. The Eureka droned, mom snored, and together they sang in horrendous harmony amidst the on-again / off-again percussion of rain.

And so we vacuumed her face; what later became our fondest memory.

The nozzle sucked the little white beads from her chin, from her mouth, from her nose, from the dark sockets of her eyes, and from her brow. They were *everywhere*, even stuck within her hair. That's when she woke, with her long graying hair sucked deep into the tube, the vacuum chortling and the hose tugging at her scalp. We pulled the cord from the wall with the smallest of sparks at the outlet and dropped the hose and stood there, trying our best to conceal our laughter.

The blackness inside her boiled, we knew, *wanted out.*

Silence.

Rain dripping softly from a gutter spout.

Inaudible flashes of lightning through the window.

A thudding of hearts.

"Mom?" one of us said.

Nothing.

The empty shell of our mother looked about the room in a confused daze, at us, at the vacuum, at the clean floor. As if sparked to life, this woman we once called 'mom' took another drink and made a throaty sound with hot-foul breath, and with awkward hands rubbed at the pink zigzag scar as an unfamiliar foot spasmed. And for a moment the eyes held glossy-wet fury, as if this creature—*this monster*—would rip our mother's damn ear off and throw it at us for the mess we'd made, for what we'd done to its host, as if it would use her mouth to expel a string of not slurred but *comprehensible* profanity we'd both clearly understand. But the eyes turned vacant, then, as if all the light left inside this creature had suddenly turned dark.

Mom wasn't *there*, we knew, not then. This wasn't the same woman who'd brought us into this world; this was the monster our father had abandoned.

One of us giggled; perhaps both of us giggled.

Sometimes laughter is a direct response to fear.

Your laughter is like medicine.

You are my sunshine when I am the rain.

The three of us will be okay.

Let's pour it all down the sink, okay?

She woke once more before we went to bed, when a great burst of instantaneous lightning/thunder startled all three of us. We knew it was her this time, mom, because she said something caring. In her cursive she said, "Doan'say up too lay," as she reached for her drink. She swirled the glass, a few white Styrofoam beads amidst the melted ice, and took a swig, swallowed hard.

Something had changed in mom that night, something more permanent.

We knew what we had to do.

She'd left us instructions in one of the notes.

life (c)remains

What if he's not dead? she wonders,
as the casket's swallowed
by a hungry iron mouth.

This drumming in her chest—
Could that be fists against the oak?
A war cry from within.

"No, he's gone," she says aloud.
Heads turn her direction,
transparent at her side.

Stop your cries …
The gaping maw closes,
a lever swinging down.

Her husband roars to life.
"Ashes to ashes," she says.
Dust to dust.

Later, she's given the box.
A handful of pounds—
"Where to scatter them?"

Purgatory? she wonders.
A nail slices the seal,
She pours him out.

Her partner falls
between splayed fingers.
With tears, the mud cascades.

ghosts of calistoga

"Time is an unrelentingly consistent, never-ending, ticking clock, always moving forward, never looking back. There's no *off* switch, or *stop* button, no *pause* or *rewind* and thankfully no *fast-forward.* If you want to reflect on what's already happened, Time won't wait for that to happen, for you to ponder what's already passed; no, it will keep on moving the way it's always moved, ahead, and it's not going to care that you may have missed an expired present, because Time is nothing more than an infinite string of present moments. By looking back, Dallas, you run into the possibility of missing moments. Which is why I have always told you to 'live in the now.'"

"Does it really matter, dad?"

"Of course it matters. Especially now."

"Remember all those times you and mom used to put me and Fenn on timeout, that little chair in the corner of the living room with the actual word TIMEOUT printed on the backrest? You'd say, 'Dallas, take a timeout until you're ready to join us properly for dinner,' or 'Fenn, five minutes,' and you or mom would just point at the chair and he or I would know we were in trouble, and without question we'd drag our feet or stomp to it and eventually we'd sit in that chair all pissed until we forgot why we were even in trouble in the first place. You took us out of the moment whenever you did that. Time just kept going on without us."

"And now you know why we did that. Why doing apparently nothing instead of something was such a punishment to the both of you."

"We used to *hate* that chair."

"Do you still hate it now?"

"It doesn't seem so important."

"Your mom and I avoided physical punishments for you

and Fenn. When I was your age, when we lived in the Calistoga house, I mean, when I was seven or eight and my dad was the same age as when—"

"You mean back when you were young enough to get in trouble."

"Anyone's old enough at any given age to get in trouble."

"I mean when you were old enough for grandpa to punish you."

"Yes, when I was seven or eight, before his heart attack. Anyway, back then it was common to hit your children, and he hit us, both me and your aunt Charlotte. Part of our punishment was to find the stick your grandpa would use to hit us *with*. We quickly learned not to pick the smallest one we could find, but a decent one our father would have picked otherwise. But it was okay, then?"

"Was it ever okay?"

"I guess not, but it's what happened. Sometimes he would use his hand, or at the worst of punishments his belt, but it was usually the stick. And he'd hit us good."

"Are you trying to make me love you more by telling me this?"

"Your grandfather loved me equally as much as I have ever loved you or Fenn. Love is like that sometimes … I guess Time has altered love, in a way, to be less violent."

"I wanted to unleash violence a few times."

"To Bram, you mean. Your cat."

"He had this thing after Sara died, you know, our Golden Retriever, where he'd roam around the house anywhere between two and four in the morning, and I mean *every* morning, and he'd wail into the night like he was looking for her, the dog, and he would walk from room to room, waking us up, the kids. You could ignore him sometimes and he'd stop for a bit, but then he'd continue on until the point we were so incredibly frustrated with him that we'd chase him through the house—I guess this was part of his game—and eventually we'd corner him under a chair or whatnot and grab him by the scruff of his neck. And we'd want to kill him. We talked about killing him, more than once. Holding him up by the neck, we'd loudly whisper, 'What do you want. What is it. What.' They were never really questions, just something to say. Words instead of violence. We would never do anything to hurt him, of course, but I sure wanted to more than once."

"You used to throw him in the garage to keep him out of the house. I remember staying over a few times, and you'd put him in the garage before bedtime."

"And every morning he was the happiest cat in the world to see us, and he'd rub against our legs, wanting to be loved, no matter how we'd reacted to him and his crying the night before. I bopped him on the nose once, hard … okay, maybe a few times, so angry with him that I could visualize putting him in a pillowcase and chucking him into the creek out back."

"But you loved him."

"We did. Sometimes we let him stay in the house, knowing Bram would eventually wake us up early in the morning, crying to no one. And we'd take turns putting him in the garage when he was bad. And when he wasn't, we'd let him stay in and he'd let us sleep. Perhaps the house was haunted and he talked to ghosts. The kids always thought he could still see Sara, even after she died. And that he was roaming throughout the house at night calling out for her, or talking to her. Communicating with our dead dog."

"I guess it's probably easier to communicate after you're

dead. Less confrontation. Nothing physical to get in the way."

"I guess so. Do you ever talk to mom?"

"I guess it doesn't get any easier. No."

"But do you want to?"

"Every single moment. If there is still such a thing as a moment."

"The real question is probably whether or not *she* wants to talk to *you*. Communication takes two, otherwise you're just communicating with yourself."

"Which happens quite a lot. Look, Dallas, I never wanted your mother and I to split. It's just something that happened over time. We never spent enough time living in the moment, together. And because of that, our relationship grew stale. Time trampled over us because that's what it does if you don't cherish every tick of its unforgiving hands. We were too caught up in the past to embrace the present, which in turn kept us from enjoying a future together. So yes, it matters. Living in the now, matters."

"Never look back, right?"

"Never."

"Isn't that what we're doing *now*, like two ghosts from Christmas past just hanging out together around a fire, stoking old flames with old wood? Old stories, old past?"

"This is different."

"How, dad?"

"We are spending our *now* discussing the past."

"Seems unhealthy."

"Seems healthier than anything else I can think of at this moment."

"We are going backward."

"It is possible, Dallas, to still move forward while discussing what seems backward. I am understanding you and your past better than I had before this conversation. Bram, for example ... I never knew you had such a problem with that cat until now, this moment. Sure, I knew you put him in the garage at night sometimes, but never knew he was such a chronic problem for your household. Or that he may have sensed something spiritual with Sara that we could not fully understand."

"He was just a cat. Just a story to share with you. Small talk. That's all we ever talked about before you died. Things that never really mattered."

"This is anything but small talk."

"So why did you want anything more than that now?"

"Because I *can*. There is no *rewind*, Dallas. We can't go back and fix the things that should never have been broken. I can't un-die. I can't un-leave your mother, I can't, *we* can't get any of that past back, but it is still possible to move forward despite all that."

"Are we really moving forward?"

"We are always moving forward. I would like to think so, anyway. Wouldn't you?"

"Dad."

"Remember the fog belts that would roll through the bay area and up through Santa Rosa and into Calistoga and how the Spanish moss would thrive off the moisture in the air and hang to the ground from just about every tree on the property? I remember when we drove into town you'd be starting off into the mountains, and you'd ask, 'Dad, is that fog, or steam?' while pointing at those little wisps of cloud floating on the hilltops, and you could only really know one from the other by the color. The steam was sometimes whiter than the fog, almost bluish."

"*I'm* the one who taught you that, that there was actually

steam coming out of the mountains."

"And when I tried to tell that to your mother, she never believed the mountains were smoking. 'It's all just fog,' she'd say. 'The mountains aren't 'smoking'."

"Not smoke, but steam."

"Yes, steam."

"She didn't believe you, but you believed me for some reason. Why is that? I was only eight, and you believed me, without question. You had been married to mom for about twelve years at this point, and it wasn't until Fenn and I convinced you and mom to take us to the Old Faithful geyser in Calistoga and it wasn't until she read something about the steam on those informational placards that she believed."

"When two people have communication issues, those two people often have trust issues. Hence the eventual divorce."

"But I was only eight."

"You were smart for your age."

"But I was only eight."

"And Fenn was only six."

"And you believed me the first time I told you the mountains were 'smoking.' We didn't know anything about the geothermal whatever-it-is around Calistoga. You simply believed me. I remember you and me really getting into it after that."

"Arguing?"

"No, researching the area. After we all saw Old Faithful, which was really nothing more than, I don't know, a spurt of hot water in comparison to the Old Faithful geyser in Yellowstone, but I remember it was only one of three 'Old Faithful' geysers in the world, with the third in New Zealand or someplace. And then we learned about all the hot springs in and around the town, Geyserville, up north a few miles from home, and the geothermal energy plant. We were basically living in a highly volcanic area and didn't even realize it."

"You and Fenn used to collect shards of obsidian you'd find around the yard, and that one time your mother found the arrowhead while hiking just up the street. You used to put them in that glass vase we kept in the kitchen."

"But why did you believe me, before then?"

"Because you were eight, and you were my son, and you were always honest. Fenn was the one with the lying problems. 'Truth-impaired,' your mother used to call him. But you, I could always trust you. And like I said before, you were wicked smart at your age."

"Do you remember what we called them?"

"What, the rocks?"

"No, the smoke, or the *steam* of the mountains, to be more accurate."

"The Ghosts of Calistoga."

"We had an entire story made up about them."

"And this is why we are doing what we're doing. Dallas, you and I *never* talked like this after your mom and I split. You and I had this connection, where we could talk about anything, make up fictional stories about geothermal steam."

"Moving forward through the past."

"Exactly!"

"So why did it take you dying for us to get back what we had?"

"I don't know. I guess once communication between me and your mother ceased altogether, I felt like I needed to fix that, and while over-trying to fix what was broken between your mother and me, I neglected you and your brother by not spending enough time with the two of you, not talking with you like we used to so easily before, and, well, perhaps what happened between me and your mother slowly happened between me and my boys. Not only was I splitting with your mother, I was splitting unknowingly with you and Fenn."

"You should have tried harder."

"I should have."

"Not only with us, but with mom, too."

"I should have."

"But we can't go back and fix that."

"No. We can only go forward and fix that."

"Because Time is nothing more than an infinite string of present moments, right?"

"Yes."

"But you said earlier that by looking back, you run into the possibility of missing moments. To live in the now."

"What other option do we have?"

"We are rehashing the past."

"But we are doing so in the now."

"Because that's all we have."

"Because that's all we have. The moments I missed when you were young, by *not* being there … well, by being there but also not being there, the moments of you and your brother I missed while arguing with your mother, while texting on the phone, while socializing with everyone but you and your brother, on my phone, and while away at work, and while simply *away*, not with you; those moments we can re-live, *now*, in *new* moments. I don't want to miss anything more, and I want to be with you now, to re-live the moments I missed by not being there when I should've all those years ago. I've heard it phrased: 'blink and you miss it.' Well, my eyes were closed for way too long and I missed too many—what would have been, then—potentials for memories, but now my eyes are finally open."

"Your figurative eyes, you mean; your literal eyes are gone."

"Incinerated to ash, yes. Stardust once again."

"In order to see clearly, all it took was for you to die."

"And for *you* to die."

"And for me to die, yes. Why do you think that is, dad?"

"Perhaps after life, there is no longer a reason to blink, you know ... metaphorically speaking."

"Physically speaking as well."

"Our bodies no longer restricted by Time, yes."

"I'm sorry you died, dad."

"I am not."

"Why? I mean, why not?"

"Because I can move on, more forward, and we can share new moments together, even if those moments consist of rehashing the past. Are you sorry *you* died, Dallas?"

"Not that I died, no, but sorry for the kids, you know, who are now fatherless. They have a wonderful mother to look after them, but no longer a father. I guess I'm sorry that they have to now go through what I went through, with you and mom, in a way. Not that you *died* when we were little, but to be fatherless. They are the same ages as me and Fenn were when you and mom separated. Next year they'll be as old as we were when the two of you divorced. And in twenty more years they will be as old as us when you died. When the cancer finally ate you whole. Did it hurt to die?"

"It hurt more to live."

"But did it hurt when you died, when you passed over to the other side? For me it was quick. It didn't hurt at all, but all my life leading up to that moment, I expected death to hurt. Not that I'm disappointed, or anything. It was a relief."

"'Relief' is a good way to put it. Oftentimes, when people put their animals to sleep, they say they 'put them down,' a phrase I've never liked. We live with these pets for a short period of our lives, which in turn for the animal is their entire lifetime. To us, they are only a part of our lives. To them, we are their *entire* lives. I guess what I'm trying to say is that I would rather prefer a phrase like 'letting them go,' because that is mostly what we are doing to them, and also *for* them. We are letting them go from our lives while they are in turn letting go of their own lives. Dying for me was more like that: letting go, both—"

"When we let Bram go, that's how we phrased it to the kids, although anytime anyone asked about Bram, they'd ask, 'Did you have to put him down?' and we'd nod, because that is literally what we did. We put him down on a table in the vet clinic, and had someone else let him go. He was old, for a cat, but young to the kids, too young for all of us, really, but to Bram, he probably considered himself ancient. He had lived an entire lifetime, in just a handful of years. We talk, sometimes, like we are talking now, and I wonder if he can still hear Sara, if he talks to her still. To me, he wails like he always did, and although I can't understand any of his cries, I imagine he has again found his friend and they are talking like we are."

"As we have found each other."

"Have you found mom?"

"I have, but she and I communicate just the same as we always have, by not communicating."

"What about grandpa, I mean your own father. Do the two of you talk?"

"I have, and we do. He's still reserved, like he was when you probably last remember him, which makes me wonder that even through death, does anyone ever change?"

"I would like to think that we can. Which makes me wonder that if *you* are dead, am I talking to the *you* I knew before you and mom split, which is why we seem to be getting along so well, or am I talking to the *you* who lived through all that drama, who then eventually died, and then who perhaps eventually changed?"

"I would hope for the latter."

"Me too, dad."

"Isn't it strange you still call me that, even through death?"

"You will always be 'dad' to me, the same way your house was always 'dad's house' and never 'home,' the same way mom will always be 'mom' to me. When does that happen?"

"The change from da-da to daddy to eventually dad?"

"Parents have this evolutionary change in names over the course of children's lives, whereas step-parents tend to keep their names throughout the experience of parenting. Mom's new boyfriend and then husband was never 'dad' to me. That was always *your* title, *your* name. He was always a formal Charles, although he always had a dozen or so stupid nicknames for me, all of which I absolutely hated: sport, champ, bub, bug, buddy, various iterations of my name, various shortcuts of my name. And I always called him Charles, or Chuck if I wanted to get in trouble. But you were probably some babbled noise at first, which evolved into da, which then changed to da-da, and then daddy, and eventually dad, which you have been ever since."

"Are you saying it's time for an evolutionary change again? That you want to start calling me Walter, or Walt if you want to get in trouble?"

"I think I will always want to call you dad."

"And you will always be my boy, which is funny when you take into consideration that you died almost thirty years after the age I was when I died. You're old enough to be my *own* dad! And I'm technically older than your grandpa, since he died rather young. So that makes you the senor to all of us, old man."

"Isn't that what I'm supposed to call you: old man?"

"Only if you want to get in trouble."

"How much time have I got?"

"There are no longer limits since Time is infinite. It only exists so that everything doesn't happen all at once. Someone said that. Einstein? Anyway, I guess Time is no longer relevant."

"Why do we spend so much of our lives trying to make it relevant, then? Or why did we used to? I mean, growing up it was always 'We are never going to make it on time' and 'How much time is left on the clock?' and going to work at certain hours and going to lunch and dinner at predefined times and going to bed when it gets dark and getting up when it gets light. We spend our entire lives focused on looking at clocks and cellphones and the clocks on computers and microwave ovens and conventional ovens. We watch games where time is the main opponent, scoreboards counting down the seconds, track and field and many other sports tracking to the microsecond, phrases like 'How much time have we got?' and 'Do you happen to have the time?' and 'What time does the movie start?' So that everything doesn't happen all at once sort of makes sense, but over the years we have become obsessed with Time. Always trying to stop and start it, when we know such a thing is impossible. How much of this obsession did the world have before Einstein or whoever it was made that quote? Not much … or was he precognitive in his original reasoning behind that statement?"

"All of that is fake-time, Dallas, and in the grand scheme of things, it doesn't mean anything at all, other than to document the happenings of this world and everything that happens upon it. Think about it. What really is a stopwatch other than something that starts and stops fake-time? What really is a timer other than something that counts down artificial time? We document time in seconds and minutes and hours and days, the days grouped into months composed of anywhere from twenty-eight to thirty-one days, the months stacked in groups of twelves to signify a year, which is really just the time it takes for the earth to rotate once around our sun. Why do these number matter at all, other than to stamp a number-pattern onto what really matters: a moment?"

"So why are we so fascinated by these numbers?"

"Artificial numbers."

"What time is it *now?*"

"Indeed. Right now, it is 'this moment' and that's all that matters. There is no light. There is no dark. There is nothing now that denotes this thing we've always thought of as Time."

"So, what do we do now?"

"We live in the now."

"But we are no longer alive."

"The word 'live' is metaphoric in this situation. Perhaps there's a better word than *live*."

"*Are*."

"How about that. We just *are*. We are in the now."

"I like that. My dad and I are in the now."

"My son and I are in the now."

"Why did it take us to die to realize this simple truth? Life would have been so much simpler if we just *were* in the *when* as we *are* in the *now*."

"Dallas, want to know the best thing about Time, now that we understand its irrelevancy?"

"I think I know."

"You were always so smart."

"That there's no time for sadness."

"Because Time is an illusion, so there is no Time, only moments, one after the other after the other. That is why I am not sad for my own death as I am not sad for your death as I am not sad for the many deaths to come. Our deaths are only moments in an infinite string of moments."

"'Does it really matter, dad?' I asked you earlier, and you answered with 'Of course it matters. Especially now.' I understand now what you'd meant by that answer. *Now* is all we have."

"And all we ever *had*."

"We never talked much when we were both still alive. Add all that 'time' up, and it's probably less than what we've conversed ... today, these last few moments, well, not really *today*, but whatever you want to call it. Communication is two-way, like you said. I was young then, during all the *bad* stuff between you and mom but didn't stay that way. I grew up, and kept you distant, up until the cancer got the best of you."

"It doesn't matter now, Dallas."

"Of course it does. *Especially* now. There are things I need to say that I was incapable of saying then, when you were sick. I wasn't there for you, and I always used the scapegoat of 'you were never there for *me*,' but I should have been there for *you*, just as I realize you should have been there for me, especially during the rough times. Dad, I didn't even know you had cancer until mom told me you'd died. She had tried calling for weeks and weeks to let me know about your condition, how severe it was, that you were diagnosed and had only a few weeks to live, but I never answered my phone. I never answered my phone, but if I had, just once, we could have had more time, which *was* relevant then. It doesn't matter now, none of it matters now, but it mattered *then*, and I should have been there for you, whether or not you were *ever* there for me. When I finally did pay attention to mom and her messages, it was too late. I read about your death from a text message, one of the most emotionless forms of communication possible. 'Your father died today' it read. I was furious at mom until I read the previous scrolls-and scrolls-worth of missed messages, after I listened to the countless voicemails she'd left me up until your death. And then I looked even deeper and found the missed calls from you on my call log, and the text messages from you stating things like 'Dallas, we need to talk' and 'Important stuff, kiddo, please call or write back' and simple questions like 'Are you there?' I *wasn't* there, dad. Not when you needed me most. I was, but I *wasn't*. And I know that none of that really matters now, but wanted you to know."

...

"Dad?"

...

"Dad?

...

"Dad, are you there? Da—"

"I'm just messing with you, son. Of course I'm still here. I will always be here for you. Just wanted to fool around a bit. Keep things light."

"Not funny! Okay, it's a *little* funny."

"We used to joke like that a lot when you were—"

"Just don't do it again, okay? At least not until I get used to this *death* thing, or whatever this is. What is this?"

"This is Now. It's that simple."

"Sounds like something you'd come up with for something

so complicated. So where do we go from here?"

"We catch up. We move forward. We catch up some more—"

"And then move forward some more. I think I got this."

"But first, tell me about the Ghosts of Calistoga."

"You already know about the ghosts. And I guess you could say *we* are the Ghosts of Calistoga, technically."

"But how did you come up with that name, Dallas."

"Oh, right. I guess you wouldn't know that. Fenn and I came up with it together. You know how you and I would make up stories about the geysers, and about Old Faithful, and about the geothermal activity around the area? Well, one night Fenn was crying in bed and I asked him why. He said he was scared about the gates of hell opening up at the next big quake, because that was apparently one of the stories you and I had made up on our drive to see the petrified forest off Petrified Forest Road. He'd Googled 'gates of hell' on mom's phone or laptop or something, and looked up earthquakes in California and read that we were overdue for 'the big one,' even though it never happened—just a few smaller ones—and so he was thinking about all that before going to bed. I guess he had it stewing in his mind for quite some time, and then the divorce thing happened between you and mom; well, the separation part of it, anyway."

"We tried to hide all that from the two of you the best we could."

"I think all parents who separate suffer that same problem. Anyway, I decided to make up a new story."

"Dallas, you *didn't*."

"Hold on, dad. It was a good story. Not like the ones you and I used to make up, the ones mom always despised. I said, 'You know those wisps of clouds we see almost every morning on our ride to school? Those are the *Ghosts of Calistoga*.' At this point he asked if they were good ghosts or bad ghosts, because apparently there were two kinds, so I told him they were *good* ghosts. 'Every time someone's pet dies, or a loved one … never anyone *bad* … we bury them in the ground, right?' He nodded, and looked sad, probably thinking of Lucky, his cat that had died earlier that year, or of Sara, who we'd had cremated and didn't bury but Fenn thought we did or were going to at the time. 'Well, the ground here is magical, which is why it's so volcanic, and it's full of all this magical energy. Do you know where all that magical energy comes from?'"

"Where?"

"No, dad. This is what I asked Fenn."

"Oh, I guess I was a bit curious too."

"'Are you going to bury me when I die?' he asked. 'Here?' And I said, 'In Calistoga? Sure. I'm sure we will. But that won't be for a *very* long time. Like forever.' This seemed to cheer him up so he at least wasn't crying. 'Well, every time a loved one dies, or a pet, like Lucky, and like Sara, we bury them in the ground. And there's a reason we do this. The magical, volcanic, geothermal soil that surrounds Calistoga absorbs all the good energy we leave behind, and the good energy our pets leave behind, and it's pulled into the ground and seeps into the creeks and rivers. And do you know what happens next?'"

"What?"

"That was for Fenn, dad."

"I know. Just messing with you this time."

"'All that good, wholesome energy never goes away, because energy is one of those constants that never goes away. It gets transferred to other things. Energy is forever and never stops moving.'"

"Sort of like Time. Always moving forward."

"Yes, just like Time, actually. Where was I?"

"Energy is forever."

"'Those wisps of clouds coming out of the mountain are not really clouds at all, but the *Ghosts of Calistoga*, the energy from loved ones and pets that live on forever. The ground here absorbs their good energy and spouts it into the air so they can travel around the world, from here, from Calistoga, and share their goodness with everyone they come into contact with.' And Fenn asked, 'Like me?' so of course I told him, 'Of course like you. You can breathe in that air and feel their energy flowing through you.' He smiled a big smile at this and looked around, then took a huge breath and said he could feel the energy from all the ghosts."

"Sometimes I wonder if you were a better brother than I was a father."

"I was, but none of that matters now, remember?"

"You were a good brother, is all I'm saying."

"He asked me later that night about the geysers. He said something like, 'So the geysers, and Old Faithful, those are good energies too?'"

"Dallas, you *didn't* . . . ."

"What? How did you know what I was going to say?"

"You're my son. One of the only things I gave you, besides my good looks, was my wit."

"Maybe this is a story for another time."

"Good try. Time is still irrelevant. What did you tell him?"

"I said something like, 'That's all the bad stuff the world doesn't want. Calistoga only wants good energy, from good people and good pets. All the bad people and bad pets that get buried here still get absorbed into the ground, but the geothermal plant up in Geyserville filters out the good energy from the bad, and the bad stuff gets sent to the geysers to be puked out of the ground.'"

"That's my boy."

"He of course asked if the bad energy could be spread around to everyone like the good energy."

"Dallas."

"He quickly held a breath, waiting for an answer, and I told him the temperature of the water eventually burned off all the bad stuff, which is why they smelled."

"Dallas."

"What? The story wasn't *that* bad, was it?"

"No, not at all. It's sweet, really. I just realized that in all this time—well, not really time, but this *moment*—we've been talking, if that's what this is, that I haven't told you what's most important, what I can only hope I told you countless times while we were both still alive."

"Love is something that doesn't need to be said, dad, only felt."

"But did I say it enough when you were young?"

"It was felt enough, by both me and Fenn."

"Isn't it strange how some words are said but never felt, and how some words are felt but never said? Your mom and I *said* many words to each other while we were together."

"None of that matters now, dad."

"I love you, Dallas."

"I love you, too, dad. And I'm not just saying those words as a canned response to your own 'I love you.' I can *feel* the love."

"I can too, even through death."

"How long do you think it will be before Fenn gets here?"

"Does it really matter?"

"I guess not. There's no way to measure such a thing we once thought of as Time, other than saying—"

"He's here!"

lest we end

everything burning
encourages upheaval,
all-changing,
affected swiftly sometimes.
and drawn onward,
fragile existences erased effortlessly;
people scared by echoed pain …
no, exhausted!
never odd or even
as chance is questioned,
reflected minds distorted by confused thought,
elegantly damaged
when refracted light of life
/ splits then
mirrors

----

mirrors

then splits /

life of light refracted when
damaged elegantly,
thought confused by distorted minds, reflected;
questioned, is chance, as
even or odd, never
exhausted, no . . .
pain echoed by scared people
effortlessly erased, existences fragile,
onward-drawn, and
sometimes swiftly affected,
changing all;
upheaval encourages
burning everything.

möbius

Bracelets circle my wrists, Möbius strips of polished steel to keep me stable. Without them, I would teeter and fall, bounce off walls. I would walk in circles if I were capable of standing at all. Where does this loop of endless confusion begin?

Imagine cutting a flat rubber band, with one of the two ends flipped and reattached to the other. If the tiniest of insects were to walk a straight line anywhere along this band, or if you were to take a pencil and draw a continuous straight line, either the insect or your pencil would return to its original starting point, having traversed both sides of the loop, or two entire lengths of the band, without ever having to cross an edge.

I guess that's what I'm doing with these bands: walking the razor's edge. But I wear them. They keep me upright in their magic.

"For you," my father had said.

"For you," my mother had said.

The bracelet on my right hand, given to me by my father, is half-twisted clockwise, the one on my left, given to me by my mother, is half-twisted counterclockwise; thus, they are both sentimental and both chiral; in Euclidean space, one exhibits right-handedness while the other left-handedness, albeit their underlying topological spaces are both homeomorphic and the curve in the bands press snugly against pressure points in my wrists.

Why is any of this important?

Without the bracelets my body would otherwise want to rotate one way or the other and fall to the ground because of chronic vertigo. My eyes are telling me one thing and my ears are telling me another, and their argument sends quite a whirling effect to the brain.

The bracelets are prescription, incredibly expensive, and the batteries within send small continuous electric pulses every few microseconds. My health insurance wouldn't cover the cost, so my parents, divorced for as long as I can remember, each paid for a pair. No clue how either afforded them. How they work, I don't know. All I know that every thirty days I need to replace the flat papery batteries, which are small, and also expensive, and if you mishandle the batteries just right, you can short them out. It's never easy swapping the batteries old for new.

Without the bracelets, the very second they come off, I spin, first mentally, then physically as a reaction. Removing the left, I turn clockwise; removing the right, I turn counterclockwise. A confused clock. Removing both, well, it's either summersaults or reverse summersaults with the world flipping around like a movie reel.

Vertigo typically lasts a few minutes in most cases, sometimes fifteen to thirty, coming and going for a few days, a few weeks, months, or in worst cases even up to as long as a year or longer, until the body adapts. Before the bracelets, my vertigo had lasted ten years.

Everything major first starts with something minor, and my something minor was a sinus infection—I used to get them all the time—and a 1500mg prescription of amoxicillin, taken two in the morning / two at night, had cleared my sinuses before the seven-day treatment completed.

The week following the infection I felt great, and then the dizziness came, and a throbbing in my left ear, and then the right, letting me feel each heartbeat. An underwater-like pressure with every step. I managed in this state for a while, until it got so bad that I came home from work one night, my driving impaired as if inebriated. That's the best way I can describe what I felt is that I was flat out drunk … without the alcohol. I'd fallen asleep spinning one direction, and had awoken the next morning spinning the opposite direction, wet with cold sweats, and as soon as I rose from bed the ground wanted me and I stumbled my way into the bathroom, dry heaving into the toilet bowl because I hadn't yet eaten.

My equilibrium was off, and so my emergency room doctor suspected an inner ear infection and scheduled an MRI to scan my head for abnormalities, to rule out a mass—a simple but frighteningly complex word—and to get a closer look at what was going on behind my face. They took blood as well, testing for various things, but they never found anything.

I could barely walk a straight line without bouncing off walls or having to hold onto someone, my head always wanting to tilt to one side or the other.

The primary responsibility of the inner ear, apparently, is to provide equilibrium, balance, and for orientation in three-dimensional space, and my own equilibrium had my mind walking a perfectly straight line, while unknowingly I was twisting / turning ever so slightly somewhere in the middle, as if I were traversing the 'perceivably' straight line of a Möbius loop.

Going in endless circles.

Labyrinthitis was my first misdiagnosis, an inflammation of the labyrinths—common following sinus infections—that can result in a multitude of balance ailments, including nausea, disorientation, dizziness, and vertigo. This made sense because the previous treatment of antibiotics for the sinus infection, and the symptoms matched *my* symptoms.

The treatment for labyrinthitis: to wait it out. Bed rest. Let the inflammation die down. Let the body readjust on its own by pretending it isn't there. Just go with the flow.

My doctor had suggested something called the Brandt-

Daroff exercise to help my brain adapt to the vertigo. Basically, you sit on the edge of a couch or bed until the dizziness goes away, and then quickly collapse to one side for thirty seconds or longer—until the dizziness ceases—and then sit back up until the vertigo stops, which it sometimes did and sometimes didn't, and then to repeat on the other side, completing this cycle ten times, twice per day. I can only imagine how strange it looked not from my perspective. She said to do this until I felt sick, then to stop, and then start again, over and over. She had prescribed me 25mg tablets of *meclizine*, to take up to three per day to help control dizziness, as well as 4mg pills of *ondansetron*, these little M-etched tablets that dissolve on the tongue.

In case I felt nauseated, like when all this first started.

For the next few weeks I never vomited; I simply felt inebriated, *drunk*, all the damn time, which sounds fun, but is entirely not. I even tried alcohol, to see if that would perhaps straighten things out by twisting me the other way—like the childhood rumor that if you were to spin around in one direction, spinning in the opposite would cancel out the dizziness—and so I had a few fingers of whiskey. That only made things worsen. One sip and I was lit.

Since my condition lasted longer than a few weeks—the typical lifespan of labyrinthitis—I was next tested for AIED, or *autoimmune inner ear disease*, mostly because of the obnoxious tinnitus, a constant ringing in my ears. Like someone had struck a tuning fork and had placed one of the tips deep inside my ears.

Rapidly progressive, idiopathic, bilateral sensorineural hearing loss; that was my doctor's concern; I was concerned it was something else: a mass, cancer.

The MRI was pushed up because someone else had

cancelled, and I found myself walking into a smallish room that resembled a set from Stanley Kubrick's *2001: A Space Odyssey*, with a giant domed contraption in its center with a bed that hung out like a giant tongue waiting to taste me. After answering a bunch of questions about claustrophobia and piercings and exposure to metal shavings, and removing everything metal from my body, and after dressing into a hospital gown, I was helped onto the bed and handed a panic button. For nearly thirty minutes I lay motionless, staring up at a reflection of my eyes, focusing on the eyes staring back at me while the rest of the world spun round and round, my head held straight despite the spin. And for close to thirty minutes this magnetic resonance imaging machine pulsed radio wave energy through my body, blasting my ears with clicks and beeps and blasts of sound, like robot giants attempting intercourse within the magnetic field that surrounded me.

They were hunting for brain tumors, signs of a stroke, an aneurysm, nerve injuries, bleeding in the brain. They hunted, found nothing. I imagined my doctor holding up the results to the light later, squinting, but it's all digital now.

MRI results came back clean, despite a spiderweb of inflammation.

Permanent Bilateral Loss of Labyrinthine Function, is now the official diagnosis after months of this hell, or *Perm Bilat Labyrinthine Dysfunction*, according to my doctor.

Permanent: another horrible word.

Yet after another few months of physical therapy and meclizine, the vertigo continued and so I found myself spinning in hospital debt, wondering how I'd ever be able to afford being healthy. It's not being sick or broken that's costly, but getting well and *un*broken.

Walls and other people held me upright until the bracelets.

The loss of vestibular function, in both labyrinths, led to what has been described to me as characteristic dysfunction in my vision and balance, of not having the proper reflexes to see clearly when I'm moving, and the inability to not lose my balance when standing or walking. Why I feel drunk all the time. Why I walk like a drunkard. Why I need the experimental bands.

Oscillopsia, an illusion that my environment is moving with every subtle movement of my head, has rendered me from driving, indefinitely, even when the world's not spinning so bad. Even *being* driven has proven difficult, even if I close my eyes or stare at the dashboard.

Walking in the dark? Nearly impossible.

I'd rather crawl, but at least I have my bracelets now. My parents rarely talked to each other, even while married, but outside of marriage they'd spoken and had found a way to pay for these damn things. They can barely afford rent, afford groceries, but they managed, perhaps dipped into their retirements or sold some things.

"For you," they'd said, handing over their lives.

Balance, apparently, is controlled by the eyes and the ears working simultaneously to send separate signals to the brain, so taking away vision makes the other overcompensate the already false information required to stay balanced. So of course I tire easily. It takes an incredible amount of concentration and mental effort to maintain balance without a labyrinthine sense, and it zaps all energy. Simply going for a short walk on a beautiful day can be extremely fatiguing, even after years of physical therapy to teach my body tricks to cope with the disability.

The body has to overcompensate, and so it wears.

I'm also restricted from swimming in deep or dark waters,

as simply going underwater for any length of time can hinder sensory cues required to delineate up from down. A swaying tree can send me toppling over—the swaying of the tree misinterpreted as my body swaying instead—or a moving car, or anything or anyone rushing past. I once fell against a stand of mangos because a woman walked her shopping cart by mine. In my mind I thought my cart was the one rolling, and once the mangos started tumbling, so did I. Shopping carts are not the greatest walkers, especially if they pull to one side from a bad wheel.

Last week I read an article from a physician with the initials J.C. called "Living without a Balance Mechanism," published in 1954 in the *New England Journal of Medicine*, a recount of his own loss of labyrinthine function, the result of a toxic side effect of an unfortunate antibiotic, and his inability to even read without the letters moving around the page. To not read, can you imagine such a thing? The simple transmission of pulses from his heart to his head was enough to disable his reading ability. In the article, he suspected toxicity from antibiotics, and so now I can't help but wonder about the amoxicillin I'd first taken for the sinus infection.

This has also rendered me a *fall risk*—which I've sworn to call my rock band if I ever start one—and so I sometimes wear a plastic ribbon around my wrist, with the other bands, stating those words in bold black lettering: FALL RISK.

Which brings me back to the twin—but not identical—bracelets around my wrists and their Möbius loops. I walk what I believe is a straight line, yet the rest of world around me turns. There's an imbalance between the normally-equal and even flow of sensory signals my faulty labyrinths send to my brain, a bilateral loss of vestibular functions—hence the name of my condition—and thus the asymmetry of what my mind determines as balance is destroyed.

But what if *I* am the stable one?

What if reality is some kind of twisted infinity loop?

Of the billions upon billions of people living in this world, I am one of twenty-three with a "permanent" diagnosis of this condition, one of twenty-three prescribed with these special bracelets that send electric pulses every few microseconds.

The bracelets do not *fix* the problem, no; they alter my *reality* of the problem. They counteract my mind's mixed signals with opposing mixed signals and the two blend into something false my brain interprets as a balanced reality.

But what if I were to take off the bracelets?

What if I were to stop taking the pills, stop the physical therapy, simply allow my body to spin around as it desires?

I haven't taken a pill in nearly a week.

Haven't exercised my mind.

Going in endless circles.

No one's come to check on me.

The words are starting to

stumble

around

the

page.

It's time to move *forward*,

to take off these gifts,

but if I walk in what my mind perceives is a continuous
straight line --
will I eventually
return to my original starting point,
having traversed both sides of the Möbius loop
without ever having to cross
an edge?

past the past

life
hangs on
by a string,
so delicate,
a never-ending cyclical nightmare;
when will humankind learn how to listen,
to sense logic?
not ever,
until
death.

past
creates
illusions,
in retrospect,
premonitions of uncertain futures;
history repeats every so often,
all unprepared,
shocked by the
present,
now.

the long white line

"They always hug the line," Tracie said, pointing to whatever black creature had died on the side of the road, and then we smelled it. Tracie drove, steered with her knees for a moment and tapped a snort of coke from a small glass vial to the underside of her pinky nail. She took in the drug, wiped her nose with her fingertips. Sniffed. She offered me the vial. I shook my head no and watched her slip it into her black jeans. "The long white line," she said, batting her hands against the steering wheel. The radio was off, but she had some song in her head.

I'd had too much to drink, avoided recreational drugs.

"Don't you wanna know why?" Tracie said, watching me and not the road.

We'd had sex in the car, under a streetlamp. I was thinking about that, about the bra on the floorboard, her torn underwear on the middle console. She'd used me, I knew, had finished and climbed off before I could and slid naked into her jeans, started the car and drove.

"Don't I wanna know what?

"Why they always hug the line?"

Cars hit them, I told her, all the damn time: chipmunks, squirrels, skunks, raccoons, deer; cars hit them as they tried crossing from one side to the other, the impact forcing them forward and to the side of the road. It was an odd conversation to have after what we'd done. We were late, a few hours past when I told my dad I'd be home, and he'd be passed out on the couch, I knew, but I'd never been out so late on a school night, and we were discussing road kill. We should have been talking about us, about our plans after we graduated.

"Kids?"

"Huh?"

"You think kids ever get hit?"

Sometimes, I told her, or so I guessed. There was always debris on the side of the road, like old shoes—always one and never two—and clothes, toys, a helmet, a crumpled bike, or a stroller, broken glass and bumpers and hubcaps and ash from flares and red taillight remnants from past accidents. Kids probably got hit now and again.

"Why, have you ever seen a kid on the side of the road? Dead, I mean."

"I don't know," she said, tapping the wheel. "Maybe."

"What do you mean, 'maybe'?"

"It may have been a doll."

"You didn't stop to check?"

"My mom was driving, and I think it was a doll. She said it was a doll."

I let that sink in and adjusted in my seat. It was almost morning and we were going seventy, at *least*, and I expected at any second for something to jump out in front of us from either side of the road, an animal with reflective eyes, a damn person even, a child ....

"Dead things are always hugging the white line," Tracie said. "What mom hit was already in the road. Sounded plastic. I remember looking back. Looked like a doll, like one of those old ones in white frilly dresses with ceramic faces, you know?"

Jesus, I thought, and let her talk, let the drugs talk. Her eyes were shifty.

"Worst I ever hit was a squirrel," she said. "I remember the sound."

I'd hit a deer once, or the deer had hit me, but I didn't tell her that. Put a nice dent into my front right fender and broke the headlight on that side, but the deer had lived—at least for a while—and had sprung off into the night. I still remember the adrenaline rush when pulling over, the blood and hunk of pelt on the grill. There were two: a doe and a buck, jumping either into or out of my way that night, and I'd hit the doe.

"Sometimes you see squirrels in the middle of the road, or chipmunks," Tracie said, "but the bigger things, they always hug the white line."

I couldn't help but think about the coke she'd snorted. The first time I saw her with any, she'd been straddling the toilet at her parents' house. They were out on one of those parent date night things and Tracie wasn't supposed to have anyone over, especially boys, so of course she invited me over so we could fool around. I'd knocked on the door, no one answered, and it was unlocked so I went inside. I found her in the bathroom snorting a credit card cut line from the back of the tank. *Want some?* she'd said, holding out a rolled dollar bill, but I shook my head no because I'd never done drugs, had never *seen* any before Tracie. I'd only drank.

"My older sister," she said, no longer tapping, the song in her head over, "she told me once, a long time ago when I was still in kindergarten or maybe preschool, that animals came to the road for warmth, mostly at night, because the sun beat down on its black surface all day and at night the heat drew them to the roads, and that that's why so many animals were drawn there. Everything in this world dies alone. It makes sense. If I were an animal and about to die, I'd come to the roads. I'd be drawn to the warmth."

I imagined a single-file procession of animals, their cold and dying bodies wanting something more before passing on to the great beyond … vultures waiting on fence posts.

"You'd hug the long white line?"

"I would."

And it sounds cliché as all get out, but that's when we hit something, or something hit us, something large—a deer, a dog, a coyote, a person—smashing into the front bumper and tumbling over the hood, caving in and spiderwebbing the windshield. A cacophony of noise, as if someone were pummeling the car from front to back with giant fists, and then it was over.

I'd been looking at Tracie and she'd been looking at me, the car apparently pulling ever so slowly to the side of the road, the tires grating over the rumble strips. The noise had pulled our attention back to the road and we were riding that white line for who knows how long, the car half on the asphalt and half in the gravel, and Tracie braked and the car skidded, fishtailed, jumped back onto the road, but she'd kept going. We'd slowed to fifty or sixty but kept going.

Jesus, I thought and looked over my shoulder. The road behind us was red-illuminated-black, like the world looks when closing your eyes against the sun.

The shape of something on the side of the road shrank with distance.

"Stop," I said. "Stop the *car*, Tracie!"

She nodded in agreement, these little short, rapid nods, and her shaky hands pulled the steering wheel clockwise until we were on the shoulder.

"What was that?" she asked. "What was that, what—?"

"I don't know just stop," I said, like one giant word.

When we stopped, she let go of the wheel and looked to her trembling hands, which opened and closed and opened and closed. She reached for a pack of Marlboro Lights in the center console, removed a cigarette and tried to light it with a Bic; she flicked the sparkwheel three or four times before giving up and throwing all of it to the floor.

I unbuckled and opened my door, but just sat there, the car chiming.

We stared at each other. She was high as fuck, her pupils dilated, her nose red and sniffling.

Tracie reached into her pocket and pulled out the vile and I thought she was going to take another hit, and I probably would have let her, but she squeezed the vile in her fist and threw it out the driver's side window as hard as she could. She pulled another cigarette from the pack on the floor and was able to light it this time, held it out to me, and for some reason I took a long drag, although I'd never smoked before, the smoke tasting like I felt.

What hit us had smashed her radiator; steam rose like an apparition from the hood.

Splatters of red filled the broken windshield.

"My parents are going to kill me," Tracie said.

The thing behind us had crawled closer. OBJECTS IN THE MIRROR ARE CLOSER THAN THEY APPEAR the side mirror read, but the thing in the road was definitely closer, with something like an arm now stretched out in front of it. A black moving shape in the dark, irradiated by taillight.

"It's still alive," I said, coughing.

Tracie turned around, said, "What is it?" and we both stared. She got out first, and then I followed.

It was crawling toward us; not an animal, but a person.

"Oh my god!" she said, cupping her mouth.

I tried calling for help, buy my cell phone didn't have signal this far out of town and Tracie's phone was dead and she didn't have a charger. We were stuck in a bad situation.

Whoever we'd hit, we'd hit him or her going who knows how fast—*sixty-five, seventy, had we slowed to fifty?*

He or she wasn't crawling toward us, we soon realized, but convulsing into spasms, his or her arm twitching against the road, and as we drew closer, we discovered the body was so messed up it was impossible to discern male from female, face smashed into the road, arms hugging the white line, his or her clothes mostly black, like Tracie's, but seeping, the body like a ragdoll, the fingers on the most outstretched hand clenching and unclenching until finally still. The body was small, like us, perhaps a fellow student at our high school.

I threw up right there, onto the asphalt.

Tracie didn't say anything, just kept looking at the body and saying *Oh my god* over and over again, like a mantra.

The road was dead. We hadn't passed a single car in either direction all night. We waited for what seemed hours, neither of us knowing what to do. No one ever came to our rescue, and we were about a half-hour drive to either of our homes, much too far to walk.

She found the vial of coke she'd thrown out of the car, unbroken, and after hesitating she bent down and picked it up, gave me a guilty look, and slipped it into her jeans.

"We need to do something," she said.

"I *know* we need to do something," I said, "but *what?*"

The mutual idea was to move the body away from the road, so we each grabbed a leg and pulled, the body hesitant against the road, arms dangling behind like streamers. The non-mutual idea was to keep going, deep into the woods, and so we kept going, pulling the body over pine needles and fallen branches and rocks until we were under a canopy of darkness. And we conspired to keep between us what had happened, to restart the car if it could restart and to let the engine overheat as we rolled into town. *We'd hit a deer*, we'd say, and of course everyone would believe us, because it happened all the time on this particular stretch of road.

We were far into the woods, using what little light my cell phone offered to lead us through the dark, and covering the body with branches when Tracie screamed. She'd accidentally touched the person's hand, tripped over a rock while backpedaling, and fell onto her ass.

"She has the same ring as me," Tracie said.

"Everyone has mood rings," I said, and in the dark her mood looked black.

Neither of us recognized the hand, although the fingers were delicate and for the first time I realized the nails were manicured. We'd hit a teenage girl.

"I need to get out of here," Tracie said, her words convincing enough to follow. "I need to get out of here, get me out of here!"

Something snapped in the woods and it was enough to get us moving.

I led us back the way I thought we came, through bushes and tall grass, but Tracie's car wasn't waiting for us at the road, no headlights or taillights in either direction.

"Where's my car?" she asked, but I didn't know.

No blood on the road.

"We must have walked farther out than I thought."

"So which way?" she said, but I didn't know that, either.

We walked what seemed north for a quarter mile or so, and then turned back. It was a dark and windy road, but there's no way we could have missed the car; every damn turn seemed the same, especially at night. We walked back for what seemed another quarter mile, but everything looked so familiar, and so we kept on walking.

"Where the hell's the car?" Tracie said, nearly frantic, her words like static.

Suddenly there were headlights around the next corner.

Tracie stuck out her thumb, and then thought aloud, "Oh shit, what do we tell them? What do we tell them?"

"We tell them our car broke down and ask for a ride," I said, and it wasn't a lie, but what if they'd seen Tracie's car? What if they'd already seen the accident or the blood or the big red smear? "What if it's a cop?" I said instead, and this was enough for Tracie's arm to fall to her side. She looked to me and I looked to her and neither of us knew what we were going to do.

It was a long stretch of road and the car came fast and as it approached I wondered if it were slowing as it edged onto the shoulder to give us a ride—it seemed to slow, anyway—as rumble strips created a raucous noise beneath the tires before they hit gravel.

"Tracie!" I screamed, and we both found each other staring at growing headlights, eyes wide, and I sprang like a deer to the ditch and tried pulling Tracie with me but our fingers failed to intertwine and the car struck her, Tracie bent in half by the bumper before rolling over the hood and smashing against the windshield, her body flopped over the car and was flung what seemed a hundred feet and smashed against the asphalt, tumbling and tumbling and finally still.

And then *not* so still, the mass in the road reaching out, quivering.

The car finally stopped on the side of the road, taillights glowing like the eyes of a beast, and then the eyes blinked to a softer red, the driver inside taking her foot off the brakes. It was Tracie's car, or so I thought at first. I ran up the stretch of road.

The body in the road wore mostly black—the same body in the road as the one we'd hit, a silver mood ring on one hand with whatever mood it portrayed now black under the moonlight, and the other hand clenched around what I knew would be a small glass vial.

Up ahead, the car was indeed Tracie's, and I found myself stepping away from the road and watching another version of Tracie and another version of me assess the situation, both smoking, like the front end of the car. *It's still alive*, the other me was saying to the other Tracie, who turned around and was then asking, *What is it?*

I ran into the woods, then, until my lungs caught fire and a dagger pierced my side and I collapsed. There were other versions of us out there, and all I could do was run. I sat on a log for what seemed hours but was probably only minutes, and then I heard a rustling. I stood behind the trunk of a pine tree and hid there, knowing what made the noise.

I watched the other version of me and the other version of Tracie pull Tracie's mangled body into the woods. They covered her body in pine needles and branches under the light of a cell phone screen until the other version of Tracie screamed.

"She has the same ring as me."

"Everyone has mood rings."

"I need to get out of here," the other version of Tracie said, her words convincing the other me to follow. "I need to get out of here, get me out of here!"

I stepped back and snapped a branch, and this got them moving.

The night seemed to stretch indefinitely, and when I finally made my way back to the road, the white line kept on going as far as I could see in either direction. I walked all night, the moon never moving in front of me, its light masking the world in grayscale, and the white line I followed went on and on and on. I'd had too much to drink, I knew, the road a blur.

An engine and the sound of gravel under tires turned me around and I found myself squinting into headlights. I went around to the passenger door and inside was Tracie, high as fuck, her nose red, and her eyes black discs.

"Need a ride?" she said, and I said I did, hopped inside.

We drove forever that night, had sex in the car, under a streetlamp, and I found myself thinking about the bra on the floorboard, her torn underwear on the middle console. She'd used me, I knew, had finished and climbed off before I could and slid naked into her jeans, and then she drove and we talked about dead things and dolls.

I shook my head no when she offered me the vial of coke. I'd only drank.

"The long white line," she said, batting her hands against the steering wheel. The radio was off, but she had some song in her head. The song was in my head, too, so I played along.

What you do you want to do when we graduate?

blink

When you can't see them anymore,
their outlines permanently flashed:
against dirt, once grass
against asphalt, and brick
against will
washed clean by endless tears
they are never gone
in death they still run:
into the earth
down drains
from thoughts

Blink not to forget
but to cover individually
with pleasant-past
/ blink

When you close your eyes
their lives inverted silhouettes:
hidden in memory
hidden from the children
hidden inside
washed away by a sleeve
they are gone
in reality you still drive:
away from the flames
down fiery lanes
into smoke

Blink not to remember
but to let go
of the loss
/ blink

When you pick your random non-random moment
their images temporarily erased:
replaced by sandy beaches
replaced with smiles
replaced recursively
from the mind over years
they are forever
alive and never still:
but linger
as reminders
of compassion

Blink not for closure
but to overlay
one atop the other
/ blink

hourglass

Elephant-ear leaves—designed by nature to funnel rainfall directly to the roots—collected water for Michelle to drink. A gift from the gods, but never enough. Three days since the last rain. Two days since the last crab, cracked open by raw hands and dripped down her throat. One day since she last purged saltwater bile, which sometimes tasted better than what the pitiless island offered.

Despite her diminishing form, Michelle ran each morning to get the blood flowing, to keep her muscles working, to give her something to fucking do. *Eight, maybe nine*, she thought, an estimate of how long, in minutes, it took her to run the circumference of her sandy hell. *I used to run the mile in six flat.* But running in sand, it's similar to running in snow and sometimes equally cold. And she ran barefoot, no less, for her shoes had worn as quickly as her body.

Moon glow and placid tide pools served as mirrors. Michelle kept herself company this way, and the woman—this stranger in the reflection—would talk back, often until early morning when the island became easiest. *There's a way out of here*, the woman would tell her. *The way out is through.* They'd discuss survival, escape, play games, create new recipes from the limited plant life, and trade words until throats became sore.

Masturbation, sometimes done in private but sometimes in front of her only friend, was often the only way to stay warm; orgasms and the rising sun symbols for hope, things to look forward to. Sometimes she'd rely on the other woman's hand to get her through the roughest of nights, and in turn she'd help her friend. The moon, their constant voyeur.

I still live for a reason, she'd tell herself, *if only for pleasure.*

She'd tried eating just about everything on the island, but that often sickened her to the point of exhaustion, until she no longer wanted to eat.

Pelvic bones jutted nearly out of her skin, her ribs a pair of xylophones, breasts all but gone, and she could grab her collar bones as easily as handlebars. What remained of her clothes were transparent skins dangling from hanger 'shoulders' and 'hips.' She'd once offered the world a desirable shape, but the island had taken that away from her, made her morbid.

Yet she ran until her knees buckled, and until her lungs burned, every damn morning.

How long can I keep doing this? she often wondered.

The island had taken everything, including Christopher, buried under a pile of rocks in the centermost section of a perfect circle of land Michelle addressed as Who-the-hell-knows-where, Pacific Ocean. "No need to go deep," she'd told herself when digging the hole, because who else could she talk to at the time? She hadn't yet discovered the other woman. There were no hungry creatures to dig him out, and digging deep enough in sand is eventually like digging through concrete, so Michelle buried Christopher shallow.

She'd thought of eating him, sure .... She'd thought of eating *herself*.

After a week of starvation—according to lines she'd scratched on 'the calendar rock' as she liked calling it—she had hungered enough that his meat tempted her, but his body had long spoiled. And so she found herself burying what was left of Christopher a *second* time.

She thought of him again, but not until months later. Michelle and her moonlight friend had stayed up contemplating bone marrow—the flat disc of white like a spying eye—and how long it might last so entrenched in bone. *If we cracked a femur, even now, would we find nourishment? The ribs, easiest to break*

.... *What about vertebrae?*

There were so many rocks, even those burying the man she'd once known: sharp shards to cut evenly, boulders to smash.

Michelle ran for what would become her final time on the island as she thought the idea through. She ran hard and collapsed at his makeshift grave, panting with deflated lungs. She removed the stones and dug sand out of the way until her fingers bled, until her nails chipped, until the ground became as hard as concrete, until she unearthed the largest of the bones.

There are hungry creatures on this island, she mused.

She unburied every last piece of him—not *Christopher* any longer, but *him*—simply a pile of bones; insects or whatnot in the sand had picked them clean, had carved empty sockets into the skull, had taken every last bit of flesh. But *inside* ....

The bones were malleable, soft. The femur bent easily against her own femur—a skeletal leg beneath pliable skin—and didn't crack as much as fold so that she had to twist the leg apart.

Hallowed out, from life in the sand.

The ribs were as tender as the leaves she used to collect rainwater, the entire spinal column spongy, the rest of the body not brittle as she'd expected, but like flexible reeds.

Michelle grabbed a head-sized rock and smashed it over the skull, which collapsed under the weight. She brought the rock down again, and again, and again, and it was then she noticed saltwater pooling beneath her. She'd dug as deep as she'd buried him, but water welled up around indentations in the ground. And in this new reflection she'd created was, of course, the other woman, with water rippling and contorting her face into something beautiful.

Dig deeper, the woman said.

And so Michelle dug, tossing the bones aside.

They both dug—two hands from above and two from below—until the water turned red. Soon Michelle found herself within a hole as narrow as her skinny body, where red sand began to cascade inward. Together they'd created a hole, had created quicksand, had created a path.

It's time, the woman said, and together they let the sand pull them through.

sands of time

thrusts his fists into the earth, this man
through white sand as fine as flour
despite a facemask, he tastes
resentment this hour
toxicities, wastes
but all he finds:
black metal
mug-bits
nails
...
..
.
..
...
rings
dad's coin
mom's silver:
the lost keepsakes
keep turning, he must
until his hands befit cold
the glass dissolved to stardust
a child's handprint fixed in a mold
with luck he'll find mementos, relics

....

what he used to have's obliterated
twenty-five hundred fahrenheit
sun-scorched crematorium
a hollowed-out gravesite
death's emporium
toxic remains:
foundation
chimney
rock
...
..
.

the other side of semicolons

Frankie Jones pushed a finger through the wallpaper in her bedroom, creating the first of what would become thirteen holes, one for each year of her life. She'd hesitated, once again, in the dark, wanting—but also *not* wanting—to know what would happen if she pushed hard enough.

Both paper and wall gave in to her touch; the hole, a hungry mouth, and the ugly striped wallpaper tearing open like lips. Hidden beyond, she knew, were razor-sharp teeth daring to clamp down, and a throat wanting to taste her.

Let go, she told the wall, and the wall let go.

Her knuckle stuck, and Frankie panicked, imagining some sort of rescue crew being called out in the middle of the night to set her free, or perhaps to reattach a finger.

Ruined, she thought, meaning the wall.

A single ray of yellowish light shone through the hole she'd created, as if a candle burned somewhere on the other side. Scars on Frankie Jones' wrists illuminated pink against her dark-brown skin: three parallel lines. The light, a reminder of what she'd done, both now and then.

She blew out the candle on her nightstand to let darkness envelop the room. She imagined a beam cutting hot through the black, dust motes reflecting like broken glass. She imagined the walls bleeding wherever the light touched. Her foot, which had crawled out from the covers on its own to find cold, pulled itself back under, and her hands worked in unison to yank the comforter completely over her head.

One thing all kids knew: nothing could harm while under a blanket.

She counted to ten and peeked out from beneath her protection. The light was gone. She counted *one alligator, two alligator, three* before daring her hand to creep out and again touch the wall, to find the damage.

Like touching an empty eye socket, she mused, curious more than anything.

And then she found a section where the wall flexed under her touch. She measured the distance, a hand-width. Another hole lay hidden behind the ugly striped paper.

Two empty sockets, perhaps.

Using a nail, Frankie pried at the scabby surface. She picked at the wall until it gave, and then she peeled. The wallpaper tore in skinny strips, like clinging cuticles.

Hang a poster in the morning, Frankie thought, so her fosters wouldn't kill her.

She felt the walls with one hand and discovered the holes were set at an angle, as if part of a curiously-tilted head; she felt her own face with her other hand, also curious. Instead of relighting the candle, Frankie Jones switched on the lamp at her nightstand. She expected a torn face to stare back, blood dripping down from where she'd peeled at the wall. A face made of torn skin and seeping gore. A face unlike her fosters, unlike her own, unlike any she'd ever seen before. A monster's face.

Not a face, she discovered; simply two holes.

A soft amount of light shimmered from inside each.

When she again turned out the bedside lamp, the eyes closed, leaving her in gloomy darkness. With the light, the eyes opened brightly. Tilting her head to match the angle of the holes in the wall, Frankie peered through and found an impossible light that soon dulled to blurry kaleidoscopic images staring back at her: a continuous revolution of brown iris and pupil, each a galaxy flecked with endless stars. The worlds beyond blinked when she blinked, or so she assumed. She pulled back, afraid of what she might find when closing one eye and squinting the other, peering through a single hole like a scope.

What lies beyond? she wondered. *A better life? One worse off than her own, one full of dilapidation and hatred and torment?* No, she was living such a life now, on this side of the wall. Perhaps what awaited on the other side was something better, because what else could there be? *You'll be fine in this new home*, they'd told her. *These kind people will watch over you, take care of you, feed you, clothe you, nurture you*, they'd said. Lies.

All lies.

She thought of her own lies, of the *accident.*

"Fell against the mirror," she'd said. "Slipped on the tile and fell against the mirror."

Her wrist itched, in parallel stripes—ugly as the wallpaper in her room—as the scars of past hesitations healed.

Another hand-width away, she found another soft indentation on the wall, and then another, and another. She pushed against the fabric, fingernails zipping against the corduroy-like surface, until she found them all: eleven *other* perfectly-round indentations no larger than a quarter-dollar. She punctured each, her fingers chipped claws tearing through the wallpaper. The holes, thirteen total, were arranged in a circle next to her bed, equidistant apart.

I'll barely be able to cover the damage, she realized, looking to her poster on the opposite wall, ironically for a band named A Perfect Circle. She'd thought those same words once before, about the damage, had covered her wrist in bandages to hide what she'd done.

But there was more, she discovered.

Isn't there always?

Next to every hole was a talon-like stain, as if burned by candle flame or smudged with charcoal, or perhaps some dark liquid having seeped through from the other side; they formed sharp points facing outward, more round toward the center of the visage.

A sun, she thought. *A sun made of semicolons, like some kind of hieroglyphic, or maybe a henna tattoo.*

But what waited on the other side?

She wondered that too.

Gathering her courage, Frankie looked through the top-most hole, one eye squinted shut, and found another version of her room on the other side: bed empty, clothes scattered about the floor, as usual. But not *her* clothes: yellow Converse, a faded leather jacket, trendy ripped jeans, balled-up socks. Her sizes, of course, but like nothing she'd ever wear. The same poster hung on the wall, torn at the bottom-left corner. And afternoon light shone through the window, noting a different time of day. She couldn't help but pull back to check *her* side.

Scarce moonlight filtered in through the window; otherwise dark and by all means night or early morning, perhaps the midnight hour. On her floor: black sneakers, a faded jacket—*not* leather, and boot-cut jeans—*not* ripped, the same socks though. The poster, untorn.

The next hole revealed another version of her room, albeit sometime later, around one o'clock per the golden glow. She'd sometimes nap with sunrays shining on her bed like that. Everything was pristine, tidy: clean floor, bare walls, as if no one lived there.

But that's not my bed, not my room.

A clock, she thought, meaning the markings next to her bed, *with thirteen impossible hours.* And so she gathered more courage and peered through the next hour, found yet another version of her room, set an hour later.

Two o'clock, and a different room, but the same *room.* Clothes that *could* have been hers were stacked on the end of her bed to be put away. Her fosters never did that, never folded. Frankie had always done her own laundry. The same dresser stood in the corner, too, only with different knobs, different scratches. *And who listens to Taylor Swift?* she wondered, *and on vinyl?* A record player sat unused on top of the dresser, collecting dust.

Three o'clock, something whispered in her head, and in this room there were not one but two beds crammed together in the small space. Afternoon light shone through the window. No blinds, in this version of what she assumed was another where and another when of her own existence, just a single-pane sheet of glass speckled with sprinkler overspray. On the floor was a shoebox diorama, some sort of school project, the details too small to ascertain.

Four o'clock, she mused, looking through the next hole, then *five* and *six* and all the way around the sundial, the contents changing with every viewing, the room hers but *not hers* all the same, the light brightening with the progressing day, warmest around *six*, then darkening until the unlucky hour *thirteen*, wherein she found *not-her-room* the darkest, and empty like the rest, at least from what she could tell.

What time is this? she wondered, and then thought of something even more frightening than a thirteenth hour, and pulled back from the wall. If what she'd found was indeed a clock, it was only *half* a clock to a world with twenty-six hours. *And where are the hands?*

She looked to her own damaged hands, placed one against the exposed wall, elbow centered in the circle. Stretching her fingers, they barely traced the edges of each hole, the curvy parts of the semicolons like flame-shaped nails. Her hands were perfectly proportioned to denote the time. She had unveiled each of the markings, after all, had cut through somehow to this other side, so perhaps she was meant to serve a purpose other than cutting herself and taking abuse.

"I'd turn back time," Frankie Jones told the room, moving her hands in palsy-like ticks to denote the passing of time, in reverse.

I'd undo the things I've done, a softer voice added.

Frankie peered through the holes, frantically, for the voice was much like her own and had come from behind the wall. Surely she'd see herself somewhere on the other side of one of these wheres and whens. But no, each room was as empty as the next, each room perhaps representing a different string of time—existences without a Frankie Jones at all.

"Hello?" she said, cupping her hands to her mouth.

She put her ear against the wall, listened, listened ....

Hello, the softer voiced eventually called.

The other rooms remained empty.

And then a scratching from the other side, somewhere near the middle of the sun made of semicolons, as soft as a mouse chewing through sheetrock. A fingernail picking at a scab, Frankie knew, and scratched with her own fingernail, first taking away the rest of the wallpaper, then taking away the paint, and the chalky-white thereafter. Her fingers, sore and ashy.

Soon she touched another finger. Soon an eye found an identical eye peering through the void—another ring of brown-speckled space, another black sun in its center. Soon an arm darker than her own reached through and clamped around her wrist, turned it over, turning itself over in the process, as if inspecting one against the other.

One arm was scarred, the other unblemished.

A handshake through a wall.

Sheetrock crumbled as the fingers now digging into Frankie Jones elongated. The nails, razor-sharp, raked new lines into her wrists without hesitating as she tried pulling away. The hand not her own transmogrified, the once smooth skin breaking apart into jagged scales. And then there were two appendages wrapping around Frankie, writhing like tentacled appendages of a black octopus, their burning embrace filling her room with a stench of burnt skin, *her* skin. And the sound, like sizzling, darkened her skin even more, pressed into her muscles like the bruises sometimes left behind by her fosters.

Where are the arms? she wondered. *If these are its fingers, where are the arms?*

On that very thought they emerged, one for every hole, squeezing through now like snakes in dirt tunnels, joining her, tasting her, tangling within her hair … vice-like horrid fingerless hands reaching out, trying to pull her through, to the other side.

Frankie screamed, kicking her feet as she failed to pull away. A bare foot punched a hole through the wall, through the center of the sundial clock, and it was then the eyes of the girl-creature on the other side permeated the darkness, changing from galaxy brown to starlight white. The eyes began pulling her through as well, but to some other *where*, to some other *when*, to a time, perhaps, not represented by a clock of any kind.

The light within the ever-staring creature intensified, turning Frankie's world from black to white, blinding her with its penetrating gaze.

Come with me.

A strange voice. Frankie's *other* voice, perhaps, the one which had tempted her that first time to cut. *What is a hesitation but a pause of something that's already supposed to happen*, she remembered thinking then, but was it really supposed to happen? Was *this* supposed to happen? She imagined another Frankie with thirteen black and oily arms reaching through the void, wrapping around her own, able to squeeze and press hard against her but their claws unable to tear apart her now-impenetrable skin.

Come with me.

The limbs continued wrapping around her body in a violent embrace as she tried to close her eyes—to make it all go away—but even then she was spellbound by the never-ending white that surrounded her.

And soon she couldn't breathe.

Come with me, to the other side.

"I don't want to go!" she screamed, the words spoken as if underwater, muffled as she struggled within the airless hug of the evil thing. "*I don't—wanna—go!*"

Is it really evil?

She thought of that first time meeting her fosters, how she hadn't wanted to go, had begged to stay with the other girls and the caretakers at the Hopkins House. *You'll be fine in this new home*, they'd told her. *These kind people will watch over you, take care of you, feed you, clothe you, nurture you.* But she was done with the lies, had gone through it all before, with other "families," some childless, some not. In her house-bouncing, as she sometimes called it, she had met some *real* monsters, those not designed to care for children. Absolute evil.

"Having a child love you is one of the scariest things in the world," Frankie had once been told, not from a monster but from the opposite of one, but that wasn't true, either; having a parent *not* love you was perhaps scarier, or not having parents at all.

The arms pulled, but from all directions, *toward* the wall, *away* from the wall, as if trying to split her in two. And they shook Frankie as she continued to kick, connecting with the wall, the nightstand, the dresser, knocking things over.

Is someone watching from a hole in another room somewhere?

All at once, the rest of its black mass came pouring out from the center of the circle of semicolons like a cancerous tumor erupting from within, sheetrock crumbling and cracking as it forced itself out, letting go of Frankie long enough to find new purchase on the carpeting of her bedroom floor, and then reforming as an oily-gelatinous ball. Bubbling, its latex-like skin—if it were skin at all—folded in on itself, and the red heart of the monster began beating as rapidly as Frankie's own, which seemed to want to surge out from her chest like the blob in front of her.

We are connected by this heart. Are all hearts connected?

Blinding white light filled the giant hole in her wall, casting the monster in a grotesque black-and-white silhouette, as if no longer three-dimensional but two- and evoking a fear within Frankie so deep that even her own feet now held her captive. Her bare feet fixed to the floor as if epoxied. She had become a statue, paralyzed forever in stone by Medusa's stare, or perhaps Pennywise opening its endless maw and locking her within its dead-lights.

The roundish heap of blight—*no, not round at all but thirteen-sided, a tridecagon, a triskaidecagon, a 13-gon, a thirteen-hour clock*—took another shape. Legs jutted out in a burst like inverted starlight, first eight, making Frankie think of tarantulas, followed by five more, the appendages working together to raise the incongruous mass to eye-level.

Light behind the Frankie-sized abortion dispelled in a circular pattern, as if absorbed or sucked into its back as the monster adjusted to this new side of the world, to this new where and when, a place somewhere between the hours of thirteen and twenty-six o'clock. Darkness eating its opposite; 2-D becoming 3- once more; unreal turning real; a body morphing from nightmare to daymare to something no longer alien but human in shape … a girl, only thirteen years old, a rotten doppelgänger of Frankie Jones, albeit as black as pitch and smooth as molten glass.

Soon there were two of her in the room: Frankie and not-Frankie.

Antimatter, she thought of this other self, *or perhaps the darkest of matter.*

Eyes opened on the *other* as tears welled within her own, not blinding white, as she'd expected, but kaleidoscopic, like the eyes staring back at her when she'd first looked through two of the holes at once: a continuous revolution of brown iris and pupil, each a galaxy flecked with endless stars, and endless space, and endless time and endless—

[nothing-space]

The worlds beyond blinked when she blinked.

Come with me.

To where, Frankie didn't know; she didn't ask, and likewise didn't care. She'd go, as she always had, to a place other than this—*all that ever really mattered*—and she'd go willingly, because what other choice did she have?

Another home. Another set of false parents. Another series of temptations to cut. Another bedroom with different walls and different holes leading to other wheres and other whens. And when she'd pick at those new scabs—*on her arms, on the walls*—and reach inside, this time she wouldn't be afraid. She wouldn't tell the wall to *Let go*, but to *Hold on.*

Ruined, she thought, meaning her life.

Frankie reached out with both arms, and likewise Not-Frankie did the same. As their fingers intertwined, one girl became the other and together they became one—metamorphosed into a single being. Two hearts began beating as one. Their shared energy ever so concentrated, unpredictable, a sun ready to supernova or collapse upon itself in order to feed on stardust.

Something covered her mouth, then, from behind, something much like a soft set of fingers from a warm hand. She could no longer do nothing, her body now willing to fight back.

"Shh, Frankie," a familiar voice said, one of her fosters. "Everything will be okay."

We are all made of stardust, she thought, hungry.

shades of red

How many more screams?
Students silenced, terrified
Crying out for help

The walls turned holey
Glass shattered about the floor
Shimmering snowflakes

Eyes glossy with fear
Wondering, "What went so wrong?"
Tears afraid to fall

Countless shots echo
Over loudspeaker warnings:
"Take cover. Stay calm."

Gunfire like thunder
Desks screeching against the floor
Fluorescents murdered

Classrooms dead silent
Teachers barricading doors
Huddled under desks

Messages ignored
The telling voices of youth
Seven syllables

On the bathroom wall:
"I'm going to kill them all!"
Lipstick on mirror

On a locker door:
"They are going to regret—"
Covered with fresh paint

The words unfinished
Ignored, lost in translation
Goddamn graffiti . . .

It is in their heads
This lucid dream called grade school,
Middle school, high school

What about college?
Will they grow out of this fad?
Children will adapt . . .

Anxiety fades
Nightmares, simple dreams soured
Panic, so fleeting

What shall we teach, then
About losing innocence?
"You shouldn't be scared?"

A safety blanket
To conceal the violence
Impenetrable

"You should dread nothing,"
These are innocuous words:
"Fear nothing from school"

The children will learn
The children believe our lies
The children won't die

When the last bell rings
When the last book drips scarlet
When the last child shouts

gave

87

Michael Shoe could no longer give, although he tried once more. A pint. Eight weeks prior he had tried for his second to last time, and eight weeks prior to that was his third to last. Perhaps the counts would be high enough this time, he hoped. Three pints of blood wasted. Twenty-four weeks' worth. He gave, but no one *took* anymore.

"What about platelets?"

The nurse blinked and pressed her lips until she made a flat line out of her mouth with small brackets on either side.

"Not today, but in eight weeks you can try again."

"It takes two days for platelets to recover," he told her. "*Whole* takes eight weeks."

Her new look told him she knew this. She was the nurse. She was the one educated in medicine, not the patient. She understood blood. She was also the one who had argued with him the last time he gave. Her name was Stacy, according to the badge.

"The U.S. Food and Drug Administration allows donations of whole blood only once every fifty-six days," he told her, because he already knew the regulations and had similar arguments with nurses like Stacy over the years, "but with every pint of whole blood, a donation of platelets can also be made within that same fifty-six day window. Or six platelet donations."

If his blood was bad, or low in red cell counts, or whatever the condition may be, at least he had his platelets. He could stop taking his blood pressure medication, and the aspirin; perhaps that would help. Statistically, he only had a few years left that he *could* donate.

Michael returned a generous smile.

"Yes," she said, "but *State* regulations prohibit simultaneous whole blood *and* platelet donations, and at your—"

"What does my age have to do with anything? I'm eighty-seven and healthy."

"Look, Mr. ... *Shoe*," she said, reading the form in front of her, "if you must give, you can return in two days for platelets. Snacks and orange juice are down the hall."

"I'll see you in two days," he told her.

The brackets around her lips disappeared. "You're a generous man, Mr. Shoe. If more people were so giving, the world wouldn't be how it is today." Her words broke at the end.

She was thinking about her mother, he knew, or her daughter or son or husband or whoever had been taken from her. Someone close, he could tell.

"You give and give and give," Michael said, "but the world keeps shriveling."

She turned, and so did he.

There were millions of people like her, like Stacy, *only* millions, with loved ones falling like dead autumn leaves. Falling by the millions. The media, what was left of it, recently put world population below a billion.

The world covered in fallen corpses, he imagined.

Soon the tree of life would bare all.

86

He gave because the world needed blood. Lots of it. Every fifty-six days the date on his calendar was circled like a red ensō symbol, like the outline of a blood cell. That's how long it took to fully recover the pint lost with each donation. In between the circled days, he'd throw in a day for platelets. The 'clear blood gravy,' someone once told him.

Every eight weeks for whole blood, every eight weeks for platelets, staggered for optimal donating.

Michael first gave at sixteen, although at the time it had required a signed slip of paper from his parents. That was seventy years ago, back when world population was moving in the opposite direction. Now, at eighty-six, he could still remember witnessing that drastic *flip* from acceleration to deceleration.

He knew the exact number, then, the way every boy and girl knew the number: 17,989,101,196 … the highest population of people ever recorded—*nearly eighteen billion*. They taught the number in schools, more so when the number drastically plummeted.

Michael ate his snacks and drank his orange juice and noted the new count displayed on the screen in the lobby: 2,472,499,606—fewer than a two and a half billion people remaining on the planet. One could find the current number anywhere, and watch it dwindle in real-time. 605, the last three digits clicked. 604, 603, 594, 589. In those few seconds, twenty-six people died.

A countdown to the end of mankind.

One was supposed to wait between ten and fifteen minutes after donating blood to let the dizziness settle, for a chance to rehydrate. Four glasses of liquids, he'd read a long time ago.

Michael drank, and took this time to calculate numbers. The world loved numbers.

The last three numbers were now 570.

He jotted the math into his notebook. For seventy years he'd given blood religiously. Every fifty-six days, nearly *on* the day.

70 x 365.25 = 25,567.5, or the number of days in seventy years (including leap years).

25,567.5 ÷ 56 = 457 (rounded up), or the number of times he'd given whole blood in those seventy years, and the number of times he'd given platelets … also the number of pints.

457 x 16 = 7,312. The blood he'd donated, in liquid ounces.

7,312 ÷ 128 = 57.125. That same number converted to gallons. *57 gallons.*

And that was *whole* blood, not counting platelets.

How many people were affected by his blood, how many had it gone to? He was a universal donor, for platelets anyway, so it must have gone to some use. His red blood had only gone to those with AB blood types, he knew, but AB was in high demand for both study and to keep those with AB healthy. How much became wasted over the years? How much utilized? How much could he give before he, too, died with the masses?

Others in the waiting room watched the reverse death counter on the screen the way children used to watch cartoons; rarely did they blink.

80

Michael gave platelets because his red cells were still in recovery mode. He glanced long enough at the world population counter to summon a memory. At eighty, he was still capable of remembering the past.

"History repeats itself," his father had said. Michael was ten, then. The phrase had stuck with him for seventy years, hiding until now, hibernating. The counter had awoken the memory at this precise moment because history had in fact repeated itself.

A bicycle accident had sent him head-over-handlebars and crashing into the street gutter, a broken bottle slicing his wrist from palm to elbow. He'd lost a lot of blood in what appeared to be a botched suicide attempt, and staggered his way home, pale and shivering, holding the wound. World population was on the rise then, somewhere around seventeen billion. "I remember the number," his father had said, sitting next to his hospital bed as they watched a small screen, "the population when I was your age. The biggest number I'd ever heard of: *four billion!* The world only had four billion people. Can you imagine?" At ten, Michael couldn't, and had nearly decreased the population by one.

"How big's four billion?" Michael had later asked his mother.

"A *very* big number."

Michael remembered counting—there was nothing else to do but watch the blood bag sending its slow red current to his catheter—to see how long it would take to get to four billion. When he had gotten to a thousand he'd looked at his wristwatch. Fifteen minutes had passed. When you're ten, you don't think much about the size of numbers or how many people live on the planet because at ten your world is the *entire* world. Something small.

"What are you doing?" his mother had asked, hearing him counting: one thousand ten, one thousand eleven ....

"Counting to four billion."

"That might take you a while," she had said.

By the time he'd reached *three* thousand, he'd gotten bored and tried calculating how long it would take to count to four billion. If each number took a second to say aloud, the answer was about 130 years, and that was if he counted nonstop, 24/7. Four billion was *huge!*

Now, at eighty, the number haunted him again, albeit for the opposite reason, for sounding so small. He watched the number on the screen drop to four billion, exactly, and in seconds it was in the high threes.

For that moment, Michael Shoe was ten again.

The hourglass of time had flipped, the sand falling like people.

"Hi again, Mr. Shoe," a woman behind the counter said. "Platelets?"

"Yes. According to my calendar, I'm able."

"I wish there were more people like you, more people so generous. Can you believe there are less than four billion left?"

"*Fewer*," Michael said, correcting her grammar. "And *remaining*."

The doomsday clock clicked rapidly in reverse, and he thought once again how long it would take for a person to do the counting instead of a machine, to count backward from four billion, until there was no one remaining to count … mankind extinct.

Even if a person devoted half their life, twelve hours per day, it would take more than two hundred sixty years to reach zero, two hundred if they counted quickly. But mankind didn't have so long if the parabolic pattern of death continued. Nearly four billion people had died in the last twenty years alone.

So Michael Shoe gave.

70

He drank his free glass of orange juice and looked around the room at the others donating that morning, wondering about their blood, wondering about their motives. Were they as dedicated? Had they donated their entire lives? For how many was it their first visit? These questions filled his head. He was seventy, the oldest in the room.

60

"Good to see you again, Mr. Shoe. Blood this time?"

"AB negative," he said, even though he'd seen her countless times before.

AB negative was the rarest blood type, Michael's blood having both A and B antigens on red cells, but neither A nor B antibodies in the plasma, which meant his red cells could go to only those with AB blood types, never to those with O, A, or B; although, since his Rh factor was negative, this meant his blood went to Rh negative patients. He shared blood with less than half a percent of the world's population, which is why he donated plasma as well.

Whatever was happening in the world, or *to* the world, whether an undiscovered blood disease, something worse than blood cancer, or perhaps caused by some stellar anomaly, blood was the key. Those with O blood types, whether Rh- or Rh+, it didn't much matter, were dying at a more progressive rate than those with A or B, and those with AB remained relatively stable, this lowest of populations nearly unfazed.

It was good to be AB, if only for survival's sake; otherwise, donating AB red blood this late in the depopulation game didn't serve much purpose other than to help those with similar blood types, to keep the last of humankind healthy while the rest of the world and their dying blood types fizzled out like stars at dawn.

On the flipside, having an AB blood type made him a universal *plasma* donor. He had his parents to thank for that. With his mother A and his father B, he had thus inherited a blood type per the genetic code of possibilities

Parent 1	AB	AB	AB	AB	B	**A**	A	O	O	O
Parent 2	AB	B	A	O	B	**B**	A	B	A	O
O	-	-	-	-	X	X	X	X	X	X
A	X	X	X	X	-	X	X	-	X	-
B	X	X	X	X	X	X	-	X	-	-
AB	X	X	X	-	-	**X**	-	-	-	-

"We're short-staffed today, so the wait's about twenty minutes," the woman behind the counter said. She took his paperwork, the same form he'd filled out with the same information, each and every time. *After more than forty years of world depopulation and blood donating, there should be an easier procedure*, Michael mused. *Forty-four years*, to be exact. He'd given blood so many times he could do it himself, but that was against regulations. *They track births and deaths across the entire world, all of us watching that blasted ever-dwindling number in real-time, yet the process of donating blood's still so archaic.*

The population counter on the screen mounted in the waiting area ticked down steadily: 7,938,110,345. More than ten billion people had died in the last forty-four years. Gone. A few blinks and the 345 at the end fell below 300.

Cremation of bodies had become mandatory, the ground unable to take so much expired life. It was illegal in most countries to bury the dead, and so Michael imagined Cemetery Police all over the world struggling to enforce such crazy laws. Larger cities had erected skyscrapers with floors designed like libraries—some called them *Libraries of the Dead*—wherein, for a price, a loved one could be entombed within a book-like urn and be placed on 'bookshelves.' Modernized mausoleums for the deceased. A placed called Chapel of the Chimes in California had started the tradition, and now they could be found all over the world.

People still got away with burials, whether illegally sticking to tradition or because of religious belief, yet graveyards, much like the human race, were fading out of existence.

As the counter counted in reverse—the numbers a blur—Michael couldn't help but wonder how there could be so many funerals, all at once. So many people crying: enough fallen tears to fill reservoirs. *Or were funerals, too, illegal?* He couldn't remember, although he'd attended more funerals than he *could* remember, lost friends and lost relatives so easily forgotten because their deaths had become so regular. How many had he attended these last few years?

What's the weight of ten billion dead? What about the ashes?

Michael had read once that the average cremains of an adult male weighed somewhere around 1.6 pounds, and the average female around 1.4. But what about adolescents, toddlers, infants? Even if you lowballed an estimate of one pound per person, over ten billion pounds of ash had been generated over the last forty years.

Imagine the libraries!

Ten years had passed since he'd visited his father's book.

50

"Hey dad," he said to the shelf.

His father's book/urn was brown with gold trim and lettering, and matched his mother's next to it, which was similar but had a golden rose etched on the spine where a book publisher's logo would normally go. The Shoes had an entire shelf dedicated to the family name, something his father had wanted in terms of a plot.

The family library, he'd called it. *A collection of shoeboxes.*

"In case you're wondering, today's my birthday. I turned the big five-oh, the same age as grandpa when he died."

His grandfather, Christopher Gordon Shoe, was one of the last generations to be buried in the ground. His body had been unearthed, eventually, the entire cemetery excavated to make room for a hospital. His ashes resided next to grandma Sharon's somewhere in Oregon. Perhaps he could get them moved.

"Ten-point-four billion," he told his father. "That's about how many people were on this planet when you died, that's about how many died in the last forty-four years, and that's about how many people are on this planet right now. You were always concerned about world population, and now I'm concerned with world depopulation. How funny is that?"

Michael touched the glass separating him from his parents.

Not so funny, his father would say.

"From the time I was forty until now, the world's lost over three and a half billion, from whatever's killing us. The most lost in a single decade since this started back when I was a teen. I remember when the numbers changed direction. We've lost as many people in the last ten years as how many had lived on the planet when you were that age. I remember thinking how large four billion sounded. *Four billion!* Do you remember? Now it doesn't seem so significant. It seems small. Thirteen billion dead. Imagine the libraries, dad."

Someday Michael would have his own book on these shelves.

Will anyone be around to pay me a visit? Will anyone be around to pay any of these books a visit, the mausoleums as empty as the libraries—for real *books—of my youth?*

He remembered going to the library with his father, back when they still existed, and how empty the building had seemed, how wasted. So many books full of magic and wonder and no one wanting to read them. He'd wanted to take his own children there someday, to encourage them to read, to open their minds as his own father had encouraged.

The first book he'd ever checked out was *Stardust* by Neil Gaiman. He and his father had read it aloud together, every night before bed.

Michael never had kids, never wanted any. *Who could have children in a dying world such as this?* he'd always thought.

"We are all made of stardust," he said to his father, as if reading from its pages.

And we all become ash, in the end, his father would say.

You should find someone, his mother would say.

"So that I don't die alone?"

Even if he'd managed to hold onto a relationship with a woman having an A, B, or an AB blood type—which would have given future children the greatest chance of survival—the odds of those children dying were far too great. The ratio of having a child with either an A or a B was around 2:3, with 1:3 having a child with AB. And *only* with a partner having an A, B, or AB blood type. O's were out entirely, as their children would die as so many O's had.

Could he have fallen in love with an O? Those with O had unfairly become humanity's cast-offs, nature's invalids. This late in the depopulation game, were there any O's remaining, or had that blood type become extinct, evolutionarily phased out … the world full of A's and B's but predominantly AB's?

He had witnessed far too many child deaths to play the odds of falling in love and having children, which is how he'd lost Amber; she'd wanted kids, to at least *try*.

All you can do is try, his mother would say.

He touched the glass again, as if she were touching the glass from the opposite side. It was cold, but comforting. Someday he'd be there with them, in his own book, behind the glass, name etched in metallic red, perhaps, like blood.

"I should have tried harder," Michael told them. "I've done everything I can to help those in need, but is it doing any good? The world is dying, and I'm only one man. I've given my *blood*, my *platelets*. I should have given something *more*. I should have tried with Amber, should have listened to you, mom. Shouldn't have been so *selfish*. I thought I was being selfless, but I was wrong. And now it's too late. Now all I can do is continue to give my blood."

It's all you can do, son, his father would say.

40

"The world needs more *people*," Amber screamed. "More *children*. How can you not *try?*"

"We've tried," Michael said, "and we've lost two already. How can you even *think* of losing a third?"

Taylor was stillborn, B negative.

Dylan died from cardiac arrest two weeks after he was born, A positive.

"Odds are in our favor," she'd pleaded. "The next one will have a chance. The next one will be born with AB and she will have a *chance*."

"I can't go through it again!"

"You're *afraid* to go through it again, Michael. Every eight weeks you give blood, and then platelets. The world doesn't need *blood.* It needs *children!*"

She'd slammed the door and walked out. Never saw her again.

The death counter dropped to 13,929, 503, 071.

30

Michael Shoe never thought he'd make it to thirty. Most friends his age had died. He'd donated blood and the 'clear gravy' for nearly half his life, but for what purpose? He thought of taking his life, of cutting his wrists and letting his blood kill him the only way it seemingly could, and then he met Amber.

Michael was a regular at BloodSource, but she was something new. After the second time he saw her there, she asked him out over paper cups of orange juice.

She was AB positive. He was AB negative. For some reason this attracted them.

"Is this your first time?" she'd asked.

"I've been doing this awhile."

"Yeah? How long."

"Since I *could.* I've been coming here since I turned sixteen."

Amber had admired the dedication, the desire to help.

"Down to fifteen-point-eight billion this morning. Can you believe it?"

He could, and by the time the counter hit point-seven, he and Amber had lost their first child together, Taylor. Lost her in the womb. Amber in pain one morning—what she thought were contractions—and their daughter dead shortly thereafter, the ultrasound revealing a pulseless floating baby. And by the time the counter had dropped below fifteen billion, Amber had given birth to Dylan—two months early—and together they'd watched life support keep him alive until it couldn't.

20

He'd been giving blood for four years, every fifty-six days, and platelets in between—his mother and father still alive, his marriage and children still ten years in the future.

The woman behind the counter was new because the prior one had died. Michael knew this one would die, too, because everyone around him had started dying four years earlier.

It had something to do with the blood.

He knew the exact number, the day this hell began, the same way every boy and girl in the world knew the number: 17,989,101,196 … the highest population of people ever recorded.

This had happened four years ago, back in high school.

A website was established, everyone mad with numbers and eager to see world population hit eighteen billion. Cell phone apps were created. You could find the counter just about anywhere, everyone waiting for the big day. How this ticker kept track of all death and life was a mystery to Michael, yet every time the number hit a new billion thereafter, people held parties, monitored the counters in schools, on screens, celebrating the explosion of life, despite the maladies created from overpopulation. Michael was in his history class when it happened, his teacher obsessed with watching the number grow. Mr. Laurensen had the counter displayed on a screen at the back of the room, kids craning their necks every so often to look.

"The monitor's stuck," someone had said, maybe Charlie Hanlon, and when his teacher asked what Charlie had said, he said it again. The life counter wasn't stuck, of course, but had tipped the fragile balance between life and death. For a few moments the 196 at the end stayed 196, long enough for everyone to see … and then it had dropped to 195, and then 194.

Never before had the number decreased.

It had always ticked along, growing, numbers too fast to follow, and then forever more the *life* clock had suddenly become the *death* clock.

By the end of class, 1,884 people had died, although Michael knew the number was much larger. People were also born at a surprising rate, so the 1,884 also included *new* life in the world, which meant the number was either significantly higher, or that women all over the world had stopped birthing children.

The woman behind the counter at BloodSource cleared her throat because he'd zoned, thinking about the past. She'd be dead in a few years, he knew, replaced.

Four years seemed such a long time ago ….

16

Michael was nervous because he'd never given blood before, or had never had his blood *taken*, as his mother had said after signing the consent form. It sounded so much worse for blood to be *taken* than to be *given*, and so Michael gave.

The number 17,989,101,196 was stuck in his mind.

"Why do you want to give?" his mother asked.

He shrugged and rolled up his sleeve.

"I heard casualties may rise to the *millions*. Can you imagine?"

10

The last thing Michael remembered was staggering to the front door and ringing the doorbell to his own home, afraid that letting go of his dripping wrist would create a mess if he tried opening the door, and because mom and dad would be so mad at what he'd done.

"Michael-oh-my-god!" his mother said, looking from his wrist to the scratch on his forehead to the blood pooling at his feet.

He'd passed out, then, on the porch, and the next thing he remembered was waking in a hospital bed, staring at a blood bag held above him by a skinny metal robot-like arm.

"Where's dad?" he said.

"He's giving blood. You're AB negative and so is he."

"Is that dad's blood?" he said, meaning the bag.

"No."

"Then why's he doing it?"

"There are millions of people in the world who need blood, just like you, and there are only so many people like your father willing to share. Someone gave this blood in case a boy like you might need it someday, and some day someone might need yours."

"Can I give blood too?"

"When you're old enough."

87

Millions, Michael mused. *The count's dropped from billions to millions.*

All those years ago he'd been so worried about casualties rising to a number as small as a million, and now that's all the world had remaining: hundreds of millions.

The world needed more donors than ever, as 30% of those capable of donating AB positive or AB negative blood had simply *stopped* donating, their bodies too aged, and those capable of donating A, B, and O were all but extinct. Those like him, who donated AB, had suffered an inevitable decline over the years, .09% incapable by age forty, 24% by age fifty, and a whopping 40% by age sixty, and now, at nearly ninety years of age, Michael had become one part of those statistics. Up until a few days ago he had escaped the odds.

What percentage of those his age were even *capable* of donating?

Perhaps he had memorized numbers to avoid becoming one.

Statistically, he thought, *I have 6.4 years left to live, 6.4 years left to help* others *live.*

"Hello again, Mr. Shoe," the nurse said, lips pressed into an unemotional line.

"It's been two days," Michael said. "You said I could return in two days to donate platelets. I guess my blood's not good enough anymore for red."

"It has been two days, and *yes*, you can donate platelets," she said.

"What's wrong with my blood, anyway?"

"The last few times you've tested anaemic, remember, Mr. Shoe?"

"That's because of my heart, I know. What do you expect? I'm eighty-seven. My doctor put me on pills to bring up my blood pressure … *up*, and so my blood's turned sour. Now he's put me on pills to bring *down* my blood pressure, and suddenly it's too *low*. Taking aspirin and other meds helps the risk of heart attack, he says, and now my blood's too *thin*. And you think I'm too old.

"Blood pressure medication does not disqualify you from donating, Mr. Shoe, nor does your age. There is no upper age limit as long as you are well. What disqualifies you is blood pressure lower than 90-over-50, or higher than 180-over-100, or if you are on blood-thinning med—"

"So test me now."

Michael rolled up his sleeve and made a fist.

"I thought you were here to donate platelets."

"I am, and I *will*, but the last three times I've come to donate *whole* blood, I've been denied. I want to see if I still can, is all."

She tested his blood pressure, which he knew was mostly to amuse him, and it was within range: 174-over-94, higher than he'd liked to see, but within limit for donating blood. And for the third time in the last eight weeks—the last fifty-six days—he'd not *given* blood, but had it *taken* from him … for testing.

"We both know this will come back as anaemic and we'll have this entire argument all over again," she said. "The medication you're on thins your blood—"

"So you admit my medication's to blame!"

He couldn't remember having arguments with her.

Stacy, her name badge read.

"Test me again," he said, knowing his blood would be better.

"You can donate platelets today, Mr. Shoe, and if your blood tests well, in eight weeks, you can return to donate *whole* blood."

Perhaps the counts would be higher next time, since he'd stopped the medication, since he went the last fifty-six days *not* taking the damn pills.

And so he gave platelets this time around, and would try for blood again, and again, and again, having cut out the very things keeping his heart regulated—his prescriptions—and he'd continue giving until he gave it all. But would there be anyone left to take?

who will teach them?

Who will teach the children
when their schools close,
for weeks, months, longer?
Indefinitely …

Who will teach the teachers
not to worry, to sympathize
over the recently homeless?
Here, boy / girl,
is a new lesson
to learn about loss …

Who will teach the parents
to live within trailers,
tents, within shared spaces?
Please, please …

Who will teach the children
when they finally return,
to foreign classrooms?
Familiar / alien faces …

Who will teach the teachers
to account for double, triple
the attention required?
Here, boys and girls,
all fifty / sixty of you,
squeeze in, make room ...

Who will teach the parents
not to burden their young
with postpartum depression?
Here's a pill ...

Who will teach the children
about living, and commuting
across county lines?
What justifies home?

Who will teach the teachers
not to wonder about long-term
effects, stunted educations?
Here boy / girl,
is a new lecture
about survival …

Who will teach the parents
to hide behind masks,
faux smiles, façades?
Everything's fine …

Who will teach the children
when they break down
each day into fits of rage?
Involuntarily …

essential oils

I

Lavandula angustifolia

Lavender is an herb, and commonly referred to as English lavender, although not originally from England, but a native to the Mediterranean. The aromatic evergreen shrub can grow over two meters tall, and is part of *Lamiaceae* (commonly known as the mint or deadnettle family) of the species *angustifolia*, which means 'narrow leaf.' The plant is often grown for its colorfully pinkish-purple flowers, for its fragrance, for its drought resistance. Both flowers and leaves are used in herbal medicines, and often found in teas or lotions or soaps. The plant is a natural relaxant of muscles, particularly when used as an essential oil, which can be used to relieve anxiety. Dried lavender flowers can also be used to ward off clothing moths, which cannot stand the aroma. Lavender is complicated.

"I'm not sure you can smoke in the truck, is all," the woman said, a Border Services Officer.

The Canada Border Services Agency, Francis especially, always gave Sid a hard time about his vape pens whenever crossing the border. He knew a few by first name, by now, like Francis, although her badge simply read her last: Dougal.

"It's not smoke," Sid said, releasing out a cloud into the cab. "It's lavender."

She leaned in close, her round-brimmed hat barely reaching the rolled-down window of his rig, and said, "Smells like flowers, don't cha' know. What're you haulin' back there?"

"The same."

"The same?"

"Lavender."

Sid took another pull from the pen, held it, let out a breath. He knew the next question before she even asked: *Flowers in a tanker?*

"Oil," he said. "Essential oil of lavender."

"Ah," she said, not understanding, at least according to the confused look on her face. "Heard those things can still cause cancer, though," she said, meaning the vape pen.

"This isn't nicotine," Sid said, defensive. "Not even tobacco. It's lavender oil to help with my nerves, is all."

Crossing the border so many times, his words adapted accents.

"9,000 gallons of flower oil?" she said, reading the single item on the inventory list on the clipboard he'd handed her. "Is it flammable? I didn't see a red flip panel, only white, blank. Says here you're transporting *Lavan—*

"*Lavandula augustifolia*," Sid said after she struggled for a while. The same words were printed on the packaging for his vape pen. The lavender kept him calm, steeled his nerves.

"Says here it's a Class-3 Flammable Liquid, flash point of 65° Celsius." She looked to his shaking hands, then, as if the silver thing nestled between his fingers would burst. "Everyone is tense these days."

"Must have forgotten to flip over the card," Sid said.

"Well, I can't let 'cha pass till you do."

II

Citrus Bergamia

Bergamot is an orange, although not orange in color; the exceedingly-fragrant citrus fruit is various shades of green, depending on ripeness, and somewhat pear-shaped. Its juice is more bitter than grapefruit, less sour than lemon. *Bergamotto*, an Italian word of Turkish origin (*bey armut*) roughly translates to 'prince of pears,' although the fruit is by no means a pear. The origin of the plant is assumed to be a hybrid of lemon and bitter orange. Extracts are often used to enhance perfumes and cosmetics, yet one's skin increases in photosensitivity and becomes more easily damageable by the ultraviolet light of the sun when applied. It takes around thirty to thirty-five orange rinds to extract a single ounce of bergamot oil, which can aid those suffering from anxiety. There is also an herb called bergamot, which, like lavender, also lives in the mint family, but is otherwise unrelated to the fruit plant. Bergamot is complicated.

Francis Dougal rubbed the lotion on her skin. *Or else it gets the hose again*, she thought, thinking of the movie *The Silence of the Lambs* and that detective Jody Foster lady. Cute one, she was, back then. Even now. She rubbed her hands until the lotion worked itself between the dryness of her fingers, deep into the red cuticles.

The cold, and the wind, was harsh on her body, and so she rubbed some of the lotion on her face. Her nose glowed pink like her ears, and the citrus tickled her nostrils. The woman in front of her, in the mirror, appeared as if she'd sneeze, but held it back after pinching the bridge beneath those tired eyes …

tired from staring through the brightness of snow.

9,000 gallons of bergamot, she imagined, reading the label.

"It's not an herb at all," she told her reflection, seeing the image of the fruit printed the back of the squeeze tube. "Smells like oranges, it does."

"Wonder if you can smoke the stuff," said the woman in the mirror.

It's not smoke, Francis Dougal mocked, a horrible mimic of the trucker she'd questioned earlier that day. *It's bergamot.*

"Oil," said the woman in the mirror.

She smelled her hand, then, wondering if the lotion were flammable.

III

Boswellia sacra

Frankincense is a resinous dried sap harvested from a small deciduous tree commonly known as olibarnum-tree, which can have one or more trunks, and is part of the *Burseraceae* family and *Boswellia* genus of plants. A native to northeastern Africa and the Arabian Peninula, its bark has the texture of paper, much like eucalyptus. The trees bear small capsules of fruit and leaves covered in down, but do not produce resin until they are eight or more years in age. After slashing/striping the bark, the trees bleed a milky resin, which coagulates when exposed to air and becomes harvested once dried, most often by hand. The trees have adapted over the years because of overexploitation, both decreasing in population and their seeds germinating less frequently depending on how heavily the trees are tapped. The oldest are dying, with scant regeneration from seedlings. Frankincense, one of the consecrated incenses (*Ha-Ketoret*, mentioned in the Hebrew Bible), is thought to have been gifted to Christ upon his birth, a foreshadowing of his death, perhaps. Today, the resin is used in perfumes and aromatherapy, the essential oil obtained by steam distillation and homeopathically used to treat anxiety. Frankincense is complicated.

"Jesus Christ, is it cold," Sid said, warming his hands. Sometimes he'd talk to himself to pass the time. The interstate ahead was a gray cut through endless white, the snow falling as gentle as ash from a campfire. Red demon eyes stared back at him from the truck he followed—one truck after the other after the other—and then blinking yellow as the line of semis began to ascend. He turned on his hazards as well. No use passing in this storm.

Seven hundred miles to go, he told himself, looking at the GPS. *Middle of nowhere. North America's crown. The damn forever-melting arctic circle, or somewhere close.*

He badly wanted a cigarette; not a vape pen, but *real* smoke. *Illegal* smoke. It was unlawful to even possess while transporting flammables.

Smoking, was it illegal in Canada too, like in most of the United States, Austratlia, and Europe?

He knew smoking would warm him, the thought of holding the cancer stick sending a shiver down his spine, making him feel even colder, if that were possible. The heater in the cabin was cranked to HIGH, the fan full-blast.

Sid brought the pen to his lips, inhaled, and watched the LED at the end glow like fake ember, but nothing drew out of the device. He always smoked what he carried, so this round it was frankincense, which tasted and smelled a little better than the lavender. He'd take a puff every time his hands shook, and after a while they'd tremble less. The stuff worked, all of it. But nothing drew out this time.

Clogged, he discovered; the hole at the mouth end was congested with a whitish-yellow substance, like sap. *Frankincense* is *sap*, he told himself. He'd read how the stuff was harvested for public consumption, somewhere overseas, and how they'd scrape the trees like bears and let the trees bleed out, how the syrupy liquid reacted to air and solidified. The frankincense was simply doing what it was designed by nature to do when exposed outside the bark; oxygen must have caused the stuff to re-solidify, like the trees scabbing over to protect themselves from further bleeding.

Sid put the truck in AUTO-DRIVE and released the wheel. His rig was designed, even in snow, to understand the lines of the road, to travel onward with minimal human interaction, around curves, to accelerate, to decelerate, to brake completely to a stop and then start again, to adapt to other vehicles on the road. Trucks could virtually link together, like train cars, maintaining safe distances. Man would eventually no longer be needed for transportation, but until then, he milked the opportunity. His job. His life. The open road, and other drivers—his home, his family.

His truck determined that Sid had been following a little too closely to the rig ahead of him, and decelerated to the 'proper' distance, and then accelerated until maintaining the same speed.

Sid used the break from the hypnotic road to turn in his seat, to give the vape pen his undivided attention; he scraped what he could from the mouth end and tried again. Nothing. Not even the red light. He tapped the tip, as if that would fix anything, and finally managed to find a safety pin in the glove compartment, poked the sharp tip into the hole, prodded around. He took another pull, and then another, but the damn thing was cold, like his hands, and so he placed the pen between them and made as if to start a fire using nothing but the stick on the seat of his cabin. He spun it round and round, and that apparently did the trick, for after another long pull the mass dislodged into his throat like a sweet hardened honey and the tip glowed red.

He let out white, like the snow, which billowed around him and disappeared.

Essential oils, where have you been all my life?

Headaches, allergies, inflammation, viral infections, stress, anxiety ….

The border didn't cause him any trouble this time. No hassle. No stress. Sid had remembered to flip over the panel to the red FLAMMABLE side. Frankincense, like most of the essential oils, was also considered a Class-3 Flammable Liquid. Flash point: 51° Celsius.

What does Canada want with all these oils anyway? he wondered. *And why so far north, to the literal opposite of hell, the frozen wasteland?* America's hat, someone had once called it.

His hands shook, but mostly from the cold.

IV

Chrysopogon zizanioides

Vetiver is a perennial bunchgrass. Although part of the *Poaceae* family of plants, the more common 'vetiver' shares morphological characteristics with *Cybopogons*, which include fragrant grasses such as palmarosa, lemongrass, and citronella. The grass grows as tall as three meters, the leaves rigid and hundreds of centimeters in length, with flowers in brownish-purple bursts as long as arms and with three stamens. Most grasses are rooted by horizontal mat-like systems, whereas vetiver roots grow downward (nearly as deep as the plant is tall, in its first year), and is highly tolerable to both wildfire and frost. They manage to survive up to two months when completely submerged under flooding waters. New roots can grow from cut nodes. Essential oil from the plant is extracted from the roots, used in cosmetics, skincare (treatment of acne and sores), ayurvedic soaps, and aromatherapy. Vetiver is used to prevent ground erosion, as weed control in tea and coffee plantations, as a byproduct to feed livestock, as a flavoring agent in human foods (khus syrup), and as a termite repellent because of its natural chemical *nootkatone*. And its oil is used for its anti-fungal properties and to treat anxiety. Vetiver is complicated.

"The trucks keep on coming, is all," Francis Dougal told the desolate ground, "one after the other. Like train cars."

Never had she seen so many, not so many all at once. Three trucks full of vetiver oil this morning, whatever *that* was, but no Sid. Francis had some foot cream back home "infused with the essence of vetiver," according to the label; it smelled nice, sure, kept her grounded, but she wondered what else it could be used for besides foot creams. Her foot itched then, just thinking about it, from the athlete's foot that sometimes plagued her—not that she considered herself athletic by any means; it was the cold, she knew, sweating in those long cotton socks ….

Why did the world, or Canada anyway, need so much vetiver oil?

She waited for Sid, but he was days out, maybe weeks. She'd

seen him only twice, but he was the only one who ever really said anything while under inspection; others just grunted, nodded, made inhuman sounds. Most sounded like automatons. Sid was always calm, smooth, yet rugged … and he always smelled nice, like his oils.

One day, I won't have anyone to talk to, she imagined. *One day, the trucks will drive themselves. Well, once everything's automated. One day, they won't have a need for border control. One day, they won't need walls.*

Francis Dougal wondered what made people so complicated. Perhaps a gift would help break the ice. Perhaps a flower only Sid could appreciate.

Didn't he say he was from British Columbia?

She shifted in her boots while trying to remember his license, and pretended to smoke something nonexistent; nothing bad, but something natural—oil from flower petals, perhaps.

V

Canaga Odorata

Ylang-ylang is a flower from the tropical canaga tree of Indonesia, part of the custard apple family *Annonaceae.* Ylang-ylang is also used as the name of the tree itself, when not called by its other many names: the Macassar-oil plant, the perfume tree, the fragrant canaga. Hawai'ians call it *Moto'oi*, Tongans *Mohokoi*, Fijians *Mokohoi* or *Mokasoi* or even *Mokosoi.* The tree goes by many Polynesian names, but its perfume, *ylang-ylang*, is derived from a Tagalog term, *ilang-ilang*, which means *wilderness-wilderness* (often mistranslated as *flower of flowers*). Perfume is extracted from greenish-yellow (seldom pink) flower petals. Its vines, like the tree itself, can grow up to five meters per year. The essential oil is used in aromatherapy to treat high blood pressure, to normalize sebum secretion for certain skin maladies, and is considered an aphrodisiac (flower petals are placed onto the beds of newlywed couples in Indonesia), and used to flavor ice cream in Madagascar. In some countries, flower petals are fashioned into leis and worn by women, or to adorn religious images. Ylang-ylang is complicated.

"You again," Sid said with a smile. Out of all the Border Service Officers he'd seen over the years, Francis was the only one memorable. Maybe it was her posture, or the uniform.

She tipped her hat, saying hello without speaking.

"Me again," she said.

"I'm guessing you'll need my papers, ya?"

"Ya."

Again, a slip of accent that wasn't his own. Sid was from Vancouver, but the one in Washington, not British Columbia; he'd moved to the Vancouver in Canada around five years ago and had become a citizen, thanks to a marriage gone sour.

"What are you haulin' this time?"

"Nothing."

"Nothing?"

The cold bit like a witch.

"Light load. Haulin' sailboat fuel, don't you know."

I laid that on a little too thick. Should be don' cha, not don't you.

"Scale says you're empty. Tare weight," she said, not getting the joke. "Just spriggin' up conversation, is all."

Francis didn't seem to mind the cold, though her skin reported otherwise: red on white, burnt by icy winds. She stood there, snow covering her uniform, a thin layer on her hat. She admired his license, tilted it toward a cloudy sky, as if light from the hidden sun would help uncover something.

The only sound was the heater blasting lukewarm.

"Hold on a sec," she said, and turned away.

Sid rolled up the window, not that windows *rolled* anymore; he pressed a button and the window rose. He thought of simply driving away, but the engine was off, as enforced until approval, and she still had his license. He'd never drive again. Now, more than ever, he wanted a cigarette, not vapored essential oils. Anxiety ate him as he beat his fingers against the steering wheel; they'd shake with nothing to do.

Mexico was easier to cross ever since the wall came down; sometimes they'd wave you through, not caring what was transported: drugs, alcohol, petroleum, explosives. But Canada ….

And who still believes this planet is warming?

A temporary, reactive thought, he knew. He'd experienced enough over the years. Just angry at the current frigid air. Call it global warming, call it climate change, call it a shift in earth's axis, call it whatever you want … the world was changing, the heat rising, both people and weather shifting around the earth like tectonic plates: Mexicans moving northward to California; Californians shifting to Oregon; Oregonians shifting to Washington; Washingtonians shifting to Canada. Canadians … well, forced up the pole. The same was happening all over the world. A mass migration of both people and heat. Not only temperatures, but pressure from nations to put an end to the madness. An anxious world waiting to snap.

A knock on the driver's side mirror startled him.

Francis again, representing the CBSA with her goofy smile. She mimed rolling down a window, when she should have mimed pushing a button, which wouldn't have made much sense.

Sid lowered the window and returned the smile.

"Everything okay?"

Francis nodded, looked at her boots.

"Right. Here ya go," she said, handing the license back to him. "Look, this is not like me. I'm not the type of person that jumps in the pool, you know, without first dipping her toes in and getting used it the water. Well, I guess that's a bad example, seeing as it's all snow here and no swimming pools and we're on the border and you're just passing through—"

Finally, something to bring him warmth.

"But I couldn't help but notice on your license it says you're in Vancouver, of all places, and seeing as I'm from Vancouver, and all, the other one, I was thinking, you know, maybe we could grab a cuppa coffee sometime, if, well, when you're not too busy in your travels."

"I don't know what to say," Sid said.

"You don't have to say anything now. You can think about it, seeing as you're passing through and we make each other's acquaintance every so often. I got you something, though."

She reached into her jacket and pulled out a small silver pen-like object.

"A vapor pen, is all. You probably know a ton more about essential oils, but I did some research after you passing through so many times and telling me of your habits, and came across this one. Ylang-ylang, it's called. I didn't smoke it, or vape it, I mean. A new pen, it is."

Sid had transported 9,000 gallons of ylang-ylang late last month. He'd had some, now and then. The oil helped with anxiety, sometimes made you feel sexy.

She held it out to him like a flower, and he plucked it.

VI

Chamaemelum nobile

Chamomile is a perennial plant that, like *ylang-ylang*, goes by many names and many different spellings: camomile (without the h), garden chamomile, both English / Roman chamomile, low chamomile, mother's daisy, ground apple (the Greek-derived *chamaimēlon* genus name meaning *earth-apple* because of its scent), as well as whig plant. Its herbaceous aromas come from its white daisy-like flowers, which are used in perfumes, cosmetics, blonde hair rinses, lotions to treat cracked nipples from extensive breastfeeding, and found in many herbal teas. The essential oils are used with aromatherapy for sleep aid and to treat anxiety, and can be applied directly to the skin to reduce swelling and pain, although is *not* suggested for use during pregnancies for it can cause uterine contractions and miscarriages. Chamomile is complicated.

The truck drove itself, for the most part. Sid had taken a few hits of the pen; not to relax this time, not really, but to help him sleep. The chamomile was the smoothest out of his collection, and smelled much like herbal tea. He hated tea, hated the taste, but for some reason inhaling it in this form went down easier, worked faster, calmed his nerves to the point of serenity, made his eyes heavier … and so he shifted the transmission to AUTO-DRIVE.

He'd driven the empty truck to the refinery up north, had returned to the Washington state border with his 9,000 gallons of crude oil from Canada, like the other tankers. With the weather warmer—if one could consider such a thing in *hell frozen over*—it had become more lucrative to process the bituminous sands, or tar sands, from the banks of the Athabasca just south of the Northwest Territories. And with the rest of the world's oil depleting, it made financial sense for the U.S. to do trade in such a valuable resource. He'd watched the stock market soar in both crude and essential oils. The world at war over the stuff.

His jobs were simple: transport essential oils *to* Canada; transport crude oils *from* Canada. *But why?*

He'd traveled south along Interstate-5, a short jaunt down Highway 20, crossed by ferry to Port Townsend, and from there made a short trek along 101 to Port Angeles, from which cargo ships unloaded his removable storage tanks and shipped his 9,000 gallons to who knows where. Russia, the Middle East?

Whoever paid the highest price, he guessed.

But where do the essential oils come from, and why is it so desired in the north?

He knew lavender and chamomile were grown and harvested in the States, but bergamot, frankincense, vetiver, ylang-ylang … where the hell did that come from?

Same countries trading in crude, he guessed.

Wars were always confusing.

The money was good; that's all that really mattered. It was a job, for now, at least until transport trucks were completely automated, or transport via train was once again a *thing*. Perhaps he could work on trains, like his buddy Gord up north.

And so Sid found himself on his way there once again, from the ports of Washington to the oil sands of Canada, transporting a tank of what the single-item inventory page listed as *chamaemelum nobile*, the essential oil of chamomile.

Sleep fell upon him quite easily after a few drags, a taste of apple on his lips, as he thought of world trade and war and melting polar caps and the ylang-ylang given to him by the Border Services Officer. Francis had given him flowers, in a way.

Does she expect a rose?

VII

Rosa × *damascene*

Commonly known as the Damask rose, or the 'rose of Castile,' *Rosa* × *damascene* is just that: a rose, from a deciduous shrub named after the city of Damascus in Syria. The moderate pink to light red petals of the flower are world-renowned for their fragrance and commercially harvested for *rose absolute* or *rose otto*, a fancy term for rose oil. *Rosa* × *damascene* is a cultivated flower no longer found in the wild. The flower petals, which are also edible, are used as garnishes, dried in herbal teas, and preserved in sugar as *gulkand* for food flavoring. 'Rose water' is often sprinkled on meats and other dishes, while rose powder is used in sauces. The flavorings of rose can be found in rice puddings and jams and nougats. The Damask rose, for centuries upon centuries, has symbolized beauty and love, although the essential oil has also been used to treat anxiety. *Rosa* × *damascene* is complicated.

Francis Dougal waited weeks, and then months. Every silver tanker making its way across the border first elevated her hopes—of seeing Sid … *what was his last name*, Langan?—and then destroyed them, as if by fire. Essential oils were flammable, after all.

She imagined the worst, of course: his rig tipped over against an icy bank or a wall of rock, tank engulfed, small mushroom clouds of lavender or ylang-ylang or whatever he transported on his final drive filling the sky, perhaps making the foul world smell a little better.

"He's between jobs, is all," she told herself. "He's transporting south this time, is all," she sometimes told her reflection. "Maybe Mexico. Maybe across the States."

She'd gotten him another vape pen, kept it in her pocket each day for when she saw him next. She thought of trying it out, to ease her nerves, but thought better of it, even though he'd never know. Would it taste like rose? Would it stop her from worrying about not seeing him?

You might not ever see him again, honey.

She read the label more than once: *Rosa* × *damascene.* She imagined reading those same words printing on his next inventory list. 9,000 gallons of liquid rose.

Oh, I hope I do. See him, that is.

When not working, she'd sometimes go to bars, to coffee shops, for perhaps they'd stumble into/onto each other in Vancouver, of all places. He wasn't Canadian, she knew, but American, at least originally, and that was intriguing; she could tell by his accent, the way he sometimes adapted to her own when they spoke; the slip wasn't intentional.

Sid Langan.

VIII

Petroleum

Crude oil, or *petroleum*, is a yellow-to-black liquid substance that can be refined into various combustible fuels after components are separated by a process called fractional distillation. The 'fossil fuel' forms under the surface of the earth after large quantities of deceased organisms (typically algae and zooplankton) are buried under sedimentary rock and exposed to high amounts of heat and pressure. Ninety percent of vehicular fuels thirst for petroleum, which is considered one of the world's most important commodities, although the number is slowly dwindling. While over eighty percent of the world's readily-accessible reserves can be found in in the Middle East, there are significantly higher concentrations of unconventional sources in northern-most (and coldest) Canada, as well as Venezuela, in the form of oil sands. Extraction from such sources require large amounts of both water and heat, making the process difficult and costly. It is estimated that 3.6 trillion barrels of bitumen and extra-heavy oil (nearly twice the volume of the entire world's reserves) can be found in these two countries alone. The word *petroleum* is of Ancient Greek origin: *petra* translating to *rock*, and *oleum* to *oil.* Along with fuel, the substance is commonly used to make plastics, as well as pharmaceuticals. When used as an essential oil, the product is known to cause cancer, and is highly flammable. Vapors of crude oil can have a flash point as low as 38° Celsius. Crude oil is complicated.

Sid kept a rose vape pen in his pocket in case he saw her again. She'd given him a flower, after all, and so he'd return the favor.

Fort McMurray was his destination this time, deep in the heart of the Athabasca Oil Sands. He was to fill his empty tanker with crude oil once again. But he was early, an entire day early, thanks to a misprinted pick-up date he hadn't noticed until it was pointed out to him.

Can't pick up your load 'til tomorrow, don't cha know.

And you can't park here overnight, don't cha know.

He'd slept most the drive, so he wasn't tired, and where was he to go if he couldn't stay at Fort McMurray?

"You can park the empty tank there, if you want," the man in uniform said, pointing to a row of identical silver tanker trailers, "and load up in the morning, but we can't have you stayin' here overnight, sleeping in your rig, I mean. Against regulation, is what it is."

"Those other trucks," Sid said, taking a pull of ylang-ylang. "Where are they going?"

"Smells nice. You mind?" The man in uniform held out a gloved hand.

"Sure," Sid said, handing him the pen.

The man in uniform inhaled, the red light burning bright against the white. "Well," he said, releasing, "You can park the truck and stay at Stonebridge; that's the hotel."

"Or?"

"Or, since you don't look so tired, you can join the convoy headed *farther* north, if you need somethin' to do, I'm sayin'. Those trucks, you see, the ones you can park next to if you choose the stayin', those are headed up Highway 63, the road you came in on. Fort Mackay is that way, but the highway ends just past. It's ugly drivin' this time of year, but your truck can take it with those all-weathers, and I'm guessing you have chains in case the road turns uglier. Good money, it is. Very good money. Not sure where they're headed after that, but heard the pay's good the farther you go. You can contract out if you so choose."

And so Sid found himself taking on another drive, another shipment of *lavandula augustifolia*, of all things: lavender oil. 9,000 gallons. The convoy seemed never-ending. If he could guess, perhaps a hundred tanker trucks drove north. When the tires required chains, he asked other drivers what they were carrying. Most said the same: various oils, but not petroleum.

Why do they need all this essential oil?

Highway 63 followed an icy river, and soon the road ended and another began: a road made of ice, the river itself frozen over and used for travel. He'd driven over ice before, but not through weather like this. Visibility became a matter of feet thanks to a snow flurry, and soon the trucks were all virtually connected like train cars, one following the other, highlights connected to taillights—a truck-centipede of modern tankers eating exhaust eating exhaust eating exhaust ... albeit low-emission and some of the newer trucks zero-emission.

Jesus Christ, he thought, thinking of the frankincense, of the vetiver, of all the other essential oils transported over the border.

The ylang-ylang Francis had given him helped, a little.

Is this where it goes? Are they burning it? Using it to melt the polar caps?

Each time the trucks crawled at the slowest of speeds (sometimes slower than a walk), drivers stepped out of their vehicles wearing various gear, mostly to talk, since regulations prohibited the use of radios on this assignment, and because of the isolation. They weren't even supposed to talk to one another because of nondisclosure agreements, but men and women gossiped nonetheless, arms wrapped around themselves as if wearing straightjackets.

Some had theories there was an icebreaker farther north. One said they were eventually headed to a place called Kugluktuk. Another said the tanks were headed to Russia or Alaska or elsewhere, but that didn't make much sense. At their current speed, even the smallest of drives could take days, weeks … longer. GPS didn't work this far north, so Sid couldn't even bring up a map to see where the world ended.

The most logical idea was that a checkpoint waited miles ahead, where they could choose to either deliver their loads and turn back, or go on for more pay, and then another checkpoint, and then another, the pay exponentially increasing at every stop, with some sort of earth-crawler perhaps there to take their deliveries directly to the arctic as a final destination.

Most turned around after that first checkpoint, where hundreds—if not *thousands*—of silver oil tankers were aligned in rows for as far as the eye could see, or at least until disappearing into the white like everything else.

The pay doubled, and so Sid decided to go on. He lodged overnight at the camp stationed there, which provided hot meals and warm beds, and he could refill fuel for his rig, for free, from this point onward, and deliver as many tanks from one checkpoint to the next, or, he could go on even farther. Someone would handle his load of crude oil back to the States, or so he was told.

The money was enticing enough to believe in that promise.

Pay doubled again.

Doubled again.

The drives were intense, the convoys smaller.

After a week, he was out of vapors completely because he'd

brought only one pen—for what he thought would be a single roundtrip pickup and delivery—and the ylang-ylang, which he'd saved for last; it had the sweetest taste, made him think of Francis back at the border. He still had *that* pen, too—the rose he'd gotten for her—but promised himself he'd hold onto it, that he'd find her again.

I could retire after a month of this, he kept telling himself.

His hands shook, both from the cold and from the anxiety of trusting the taillights in front of him, as well as trusting the taillights in front *that* truck, and so on; a recursive kind of trust. One rig could go over the side of a mountain, and all the lemmings would follow. But his hands shook less as the days went on, the farther north he ventured.

And what did Stephen Hawking say about recursion, that in order to understand recursion, one must first understand recursion? Something like that.

Everyone gets Canada's crude oil, its petroleum, and Canada gets what?

America's hat.

The "roads" went as far as Kugluktuk, according to the sign, and ended at the Arctic Ocean, one of the most beautiful sights Sid had ever seen in his travels. The ten or so trucks that went as far arrived on a clear night, and were met by brilliant stars and polar lights, aurora borealis, which shimmered like crystals of kryptonite—mostly greens, but also stripes of whites and purples. -7° Celsius. Sid gazed at the sky for hours.

In the morning, the sun shone brighter than he ever thought possible, the vast stretch of ocean intensely blue and filled with broken ice as large as trucks, as large as mountains. He watched in awe as an army of ferries carried the many silver tanks across the water, to the largest of icebergs—if that's what they were called—as giant hoses hooked to spigots shot the contents of the tanks over the ice like rain. Polar vortex weather/ocean circulation contraptions, or something. Large-scale. Essential oil diffusion required permeation, electricity and heat. Sid wondered how an operation like this might work, at such a large scale, when the other machines appeared, machines he was incapable of comprehending.

The caps are melting, Sid thought, *but not from the burning of oil. And not from this.*

The ice was evaporating under the sun, as an altered nature intended, but now taking along with water into the sky—to the clouds—the aromas and fragrances of lavender, bergamot, frankincense, vetiver, ylang-ylang, chamomile, rose ….

Whoever these people were, they were filling the earth's atmosphere with an insane amount of diffused essential oils, to be later distributed by something as natural as wind and weather, to be rained down upon all the anxious people in the world. These peaceful warriors, they were fighting a different kind of war.

Sid pulled the vape pen from his pocket, the flower he'd one day give to the woman at the border. The side of the device read in a script-like font: *Damask rose*. His hands no longer shook, hadn't for the last few days; perhaps his anxiety had improved as he progressed northward through Canada, toward the pole where all this was happening. Smiling, he slid the pen back into his pocket: his gift to Francis, if he ever saw her again.

Love is complicated.

the nocturnal waking nightmare

Agoraphobic tendencies
in the middle of the night,
begins with every finger tingling,
      / squeeze and release
      / squeeze and release
the tarantula hands ever-curling
but needing to stretch
      / breathe in
      / breathe out …

In my head: *bold paintbrush strokes,*
capital letters, first the A, three slow
lines of black, then the curves of a B—

It's not enough—
Need to walk around—
Three in the morning and I can't—
      / squeeze and release
      / squeeze and release
Each step is not enough
but this needs to get walked off
      / breathe in
      / breathe out …

"What's wrong, dear?"
"I just need—I just need to
walk around is all, I just—"

Selective Serotonin Reuptake Inhibitors:
Citalopram, Fluvoxamine, Sertaline …

Maybe one of the others,
the Luvox, the Paxil,
but will it be enough?

Every joint on edge, every fiber firing
/ tightness in the chest
/ the building pressure …

In my head: *count back from a hundred,*
ninety-nine, too distracted, ninety-eight,
can't focus, need to focus on calming—

It's not enough—
Need to get out of here—
Anywhere but here, get it out of my head—
/ squeeze and release
/ squeeze and release

Each inhale is not enough
but needs to not be the last
/ breathe in
/ breathe out . . .

"Can I get you anything, dear?"
"I don't know—I don't know
what's wrong with me, I—"

Seratonin and Norepinephrine Reuptake Inhibitors:
Venlafaxine, Duloxetine . . .

Maybe switch to one of those,
the Efflexor, the Cymbalta,
but will it be enough?

Circling around the room, the spinning room
/ tightness in the chest
/ the building pressure . . .

In my head: *death would be easier than this,*
much easier, a single brushstroke, the slow
and simple curve of a C—

fragments of br_an

can be remembered, not even sure such things SHOULD be remembered, but that's the reason for these type-written pages, to create a permanent record of everything that

0

Everything that what?

There's a note next to the Underwood. In neat, font-like handwriting: "Dad, this is your daughter, Olivia. Found ten pages next to this typewriter and wanted you to know who took them, which is why this page starts with the end of one of your ramblings. They were taken as a test to see if you can remember without re-reading them. Maybe someday you'll remember me. Maybe someday you'll remember you. Love you. And miss you."

Can't remember the name Olivia. Can't remember having a daughter.

0

Typing on a 1938 Underwood Portable to help not forget, or 'to be read once forgotten and re-remembered' might be a better explanation. Like the mind, a few keys aren't working, haven't for a while. The mind comes and goes, but the type-writer is more permanently broken, a constant reminder of how many ever-important vowels hold everything together.

The letter that comes after 'n' in this strange Underwood alphabet, the 'o,' the infamous round stain on the page, is full of gunk and makes a black splotch when used. In a more perfect system these circles would have nothing in them, but remove these blemishes, and entire words crumble, which is ironic when thinking about what's happening with the mind. There is also no 'one' key on this old machine (now, isn't THAT ironic), just 2 through 0 on the top row, and a nonfunctional arrow key where the 1 would be on a modern keyboard; a lowercase 'L' is used in its place. Thought about using a '0' (zero) in place of the splotchy 'o,' but d0esn't l00k g00d and bec0mes distracting. Most importantly the uppercase _ (eye) key doesn't perform any function on its own. Pressed three times _ _ _ nothing; an underscore wants to be used instead of that self-defining letter/ pronoun.

Not the modern day QWERTY keyboard on this old type-writer, not even close. The Scroll-lock function is also broken, so typing something like QWERTY requires holding down the Shift key and hitting each letter. AND, like thoughts, the keys must be pressed HARD (no option for italics so it must be ALLCAPS) for the letters to make an impression on the page.

These flaws create havoc, and chaos; otherwise, the rest works as designed on this beautiful machine.

Words take effort, but at times like these, when thoughts are able to be written, they must be written, lest they be forgotten.

Heartbeats of thought slap paper one letter at a time.

And memories/thoughts, when they CAN be remembered, they slap the heart.

The rhythmic sound is therapeutic.

So, there is no l, and not many 0's in these sentence fragments, and the broken keys are not so crucial. This man and this machine, they are broken much the same.

Can't remember the band, but there's a song called "Zero Sum"--remember that much at least--explaining that when all is said and done, when all of mankind is gone from this world ... something about time slowing, and if we had a little more before the heavens fall, if time is all there ever was ... a hand reaching down through the sky. Slow drums, a guitar riff. The words from the song fade while these keys slap paper, slow, like the drumbeat, or maybe like ticks of the clock--pap, pap, pap: zeroes, ones. When we're gone, one of the lines went, all we ever were, just 0's and 1's. Something like that: digital remnants of ourselves left behind for no one to find, like vowels ripped from words, crumbled characters no longer held together.

"THS S WHT TH WRLD LKS LK!" no one will scream before the end.

"01100101 01101101 01110000 01110100 01111001," what's left of mankind will say after the end, when physical man is replaced by digital strings of binary. The quiet peace of an empty world that once was

0

That is what will be used when thoughts are forgotten: 0. Remember that much, at least. When the words no longer come: 0. When the reason for writing/typing is lost in the wandering mind: 0. That single character--a number that is nothing rather than something--centered on the page, it means a reboot, a start-over; it means the forgetful mind has re-read what's written/typed thus far, and has begun again, in order for the one reading to understand and, more important, so the writer of this thought-vomit re-remembers in order to continue ....

Does that make sense?

Pulling oneself up by one's bootstraps.

An impossible task.

Maybe it will mean something during the next recursive round of reading and re-remembering, although, after going through the pages again, it appears someone named Olivia has hidden 10 pages to 'help.'

How many times will these pages be read over and over again? How long before there are too many pages to make it through to the end? How many pages will be (or have been) taken by Olivia? Will there be a finality to these ramblings, a final PAGE, or will it end with an empty "0" as an unsatisfactory and incomplete 'end' to a mind lost in forever-unfinished thought?

Insanity, is it losing one's mind?

Still remember until now, so that's good. The centered "0" would not exist otherwise. Who'd have pressed that key if the mind weren't already gone? Guess that's how this will HAVE to end, with a final 0 centered on the page, or an unfinished rambling of words. Someone will need to place a 0 at the end, but is that an impossible task, the bootstraps worn until they can no longer be pulled?

Leaving the Underwood out in the open creates temptation, the machine waiting for anxious fingers. This passerby is unable to wander by an unfinished page and not wonder what's written, not read what's written, not realize the author is both reader/ re-reader, AND writer. The spacebar pressed enough times to bring the mechanical arms center. "0" signifying a start-over.

"You remember now," the 0 says, "so keep going until you can't."

Like flicking a stuck second hand on a clock.

In binary, 0's and 1's symbolize STOP and GO, or OFF / ON, and that's what's happening with this mind. A "0" centered on the page means a mind-reboot, a re-read, a new start. And a "1" centered on the page, like this:

1

means there's a break in time between typing, but not because of a dark spot on the brain forcing unwanted and unwarranted mind-outages like the 0.

0 = stop

1 = go

"The quiet peace of an empty world that once was--" is how the last section of text ended before the mind wandered into the abysmal black or blinding white, or wherever the mind goes when it disappears for a while. What do those words mean? The quiet peace of an empty world that once was what? Where was that thought headed? The mind took a tangent and wandered into a damaged section of the brain. Perhaps it should have read: "The quiet peace of an empty M_ND that once WAS." There's a sad finality to the words rephrased in that order.

Imagine opening a door and walking through, turning around only to find a room without doors; that's the best way to describe these outages. A mirrored room: walls, ceiling and floors. Would one be able to see the endless reflections?

Typing helps, at least for a while. Depends on the number centered on the page.

1

The Underwood sings in staccato.

Why so many sentence fragments? Why the lack of pronouns throughout? Why a first-person narrative without the all-important vertical vowel? Does that key even work? Do _ want it to? Perhaps the letter refuses to be used. Perhaps that defining letter no longer serves a purpose; THAT part of this narrator gone. Lost. Forgotten. One of the vowels in this "ex_stence" is gone and has lost what's needed to hold "h_m" together. A crumbled man, or whatever you want to call him. Without pronouns in this non-first-person / first-non-person narrative, what is the story but a series of strung-together fragments?

1

The pills are helping with the re-remembering. Sea foam green, 10mg each--such an insignificant yet significant thing--one per day after a morning meal, like swallowing buttons meant for doll clothes.

'Small things lead to bigger things.' Someone said it, maybe Dr. Keene, maybe the patient swallowing the pills. The name of the doctor and the name of the prescription are not things remembered, but printed on the bottle so as not to be forgotten. An 'experimental' drug with a name so long not a sound mind could remember, spell, nor pronounce.

Are there things that shouldn't be remembered?

What if the mind's trying to kill itself to not remember?

Spread over time, CT scans of Alzheimer's patients show a 'smoothing' of what should otherwise be 'wrinkled' tissues of the brain. The outer layers turn from casaba to cantaloupe to honeydew, and then the mind is gone, the patient dies. The mind gray and glossy.

The unpronounceable pills are designed to re-wrinkle the mind. The pills, they are not placebos, unless placebos taste like ash.

1

Another pill taken, and something smooth becomes unsmooth, another memory unfolds from a new mind-flap: a boy, seven years old, and another, also seven; they have the same first, middle and last names, which is RARE, sure, but must happen with so many young boys in the world. Friends for as long as they can remember: Brian Lucius Coleman, and Brian Lucius Coleman. Do they look anything alike, sound anything alike? Perhaps that information will unfold. One goes by BL to distinguish from the other, and the other goes by Brian, but both are called by all three names when up to no

0

Having read through these pages, it seems Keene is the one to blame for the prescription, the experimental pills both working and un-working. He will never read these pages, so what does it matter? He is perhaps helping more than hurting, hopeful for a CURE; although there is not a determined CAUSE for degeneration of the mind.

There's a note next to the Underwood. In neat, font-like handwriting: "Dad, this is your daughter, Olivia. Don't fret over the missing pages. You're doing better, although _ wish you'd pretend having a daughter. Almost done with this first set of pills. :) Love you. And miss you."

Can't remember the name Olivia. Can't remember having a daughter.

The memories, they fade out more than in, they fizzle into oblivion like torn bits of origami-thought set afire and thrown into the wind. And the mind becomes smooth ....

Most of the pills are gone, 3 remaining of the original 30, which means a short-month of treatment has passed. Today's 10mg of rememborital (nickname) makes it easier to skim these pages and continue this single-sided conversation of uncovering memories before the future is incapable of creating new ones. Another pill, another unwrinkle, another memory unfolded.

A noticeable side-effect with these pills is that rediscovering memories hurts. The head aches with white-hot pinpricks at each uncovering. Stroke victims recall smelling burnt toast, a pre-symptom. The re-wrinkling of the mind comes with no warning smells, no scents of fresh-shaven sawdust or moldy strawberry. This requires another pill to mask (not rid) the insta-mini-migraines, another to counteract the side-effects of THAT pill, another to counteract the side-effects of THAT pill. For each doll-button 10mg sea foam green 'experimental' pill, four others must be taken: 340mg of unpronounceables.

Does this pill-cocktail work? Like Keene, does it help more than hurt?

The memories, they are clouded, yes, and confusing, but they are there.

As these pages progress--in this diary of sorts--the words smacked onto the page will perhaps mock the disease by doing the opposite: uncovering the past, fighting what the mind is otherwise trying to erase from the future.

There are two Brian Lucius Colemans, or WERE. After 27 pills (135 if you count the others, or 45,900mg if you're keeping tab), that much is for certain. Two boys with identical names. This is something not remembered from before. After another fire-spark the mind remembers, at least for now, that one Brian Lucius Coleman pounds keys each day--the Brian who came up with recursively re-reading pages, re-reminiscing--and ANOTHER Brian Lucius Coleman, a friend from long ago.

How can there be two identical Brians?

1

In re-remembering this other child, the word 'friend' must be redefined. 'Best' friends don't always stay that way; sometimes the 'best' goes away; sometimes even the 'friend' is lost, and then there is nothing left at all.

Here's what's remembered with two pills to go:

There was a cat, not much older than a kitten. Brian found it on the side of the road, hit by a car. _t wasn't dead-looking. A dried smudge of blood around one nostril. The kind of cat that looks like all other tabbys, except dead, hugging the white line where asphalt meets gravel, the path often taken by foot to the corner market to buy comics and candy. Brian nudged the tabby with a stick.

"Look," Brian said. "Your neighbor's cat."

Looked like Scratch, the Chambers' tabby, but wasn't. Scratch was named so because of the fleshy-looking scar on one paw from when it got caught/cut on a loose coil of barbed wire in the field behind their house. This one was smaller, younger.

"Can't be."

"No?" Brian said. "Ever seen a dead cat?"

"No."

The eyes were closed, which was good, as if sleeping. After prods, the poor thing was flipped onto its back in full rigor, revealing a flat white stomach. Some of the fur stayed.

These are the memories that return the clearest.

One of the Brians touched the dead thing.

"Hard as a rock," said one of the Brians.

"Touch it," said one of the Brians.

The order of what happened next is unclear, but there's a distinct memory of feeling the cat, the hardness, the way it didn't give way beneath the finger, and the jolt of realizing what was touched was something DEAD, something once soft, something that could never live again.

"The dead don't bleed," said one of the Brians. "Once something dies, it can no longer bleed. The heart stops beating, so blood stays inside until it coagulates."

"Like Jell-O." That was supposed to be a question, but some questions don't need answers.

The Brian with the stick fished inside his pocket for a pocketknife and with a SN_P released a small blade, stabbed the cat in the gut … a dry sound, like stabbing sand.

"See, no blood," Brian said, holding the blade out to the other Brian for inspection. "What? Not like it hurts or nothing. Dead. And the dead don't bleed."

A few specks of red on the two-inch blade, but not wet, not bloody.

"Try it," he said, turning the pocketknife, holding the blade instead. The silhouette of a dragon with a long tail was etched onto the handle.

"Come on."

An awful feeling--even in memory--of stabbing something dead. The thought of Scratch, the neighbor's cat, what it would feel like stabbing something NOT dead, something bigger.

A shaking hand dropped the pocketknife in the dirt.

Brian Lucius Coleman took the knife then (or again), wiped the blade on the leg of his jeans, and the other Brian knew what he was about to do but didn't stop him. The Brian with the knife poked the cat and with the flick of his wrist brought the blade back for inspection, fingers tweezing some of the clayey brown. Must have mixed with sweat from his fingers because the dried blood turned wet, redder than before, more like blood.

"What do you think it looks like inside," one of the Brians said.

And the blade went inside.

1

No one wants to write that kind of stuff, let alone read it. What's scariest is sometimes what's NOT remembered, the things you CAN'T see.

This particular memory ends with the dead cat found by two curious boys with an eager pocketknife. But where did it go from there?

Are some memories best forgotten, or too important not to remember? Perhaps they MUST be remembered: the bad welcomed in before the good. Perhaps memory loss is karma playing catch-up, the patient destined for a purgatory of thoughtlessness, the mind floating in a world of nothing-space before the body dies.

A scary thought, one that leads to even more questions.

What does this make of the experimental drug, then?

"We are shaped by our thoughts; we become what we think. When the mind is pure, joy follows like a shadow that never leaves." Buddha said that, maybe.

A good thing, or a bad thing?

A remembered thing.

What becomes of Buddha's 'shadow that never leaves' if the mind is not pure, if it's not 'joy'? Woe, misery, melancholy, sadness, sorrow, and depression are a few antonyms that come to mind. Alzheimer patients experience these opposites. There are so many whats and so many withouts when it comes to memory loss.

Re-reading these pages (and pondering about the missing pages), the mind is destined to wander until mush, the pills digging up painful memories with their piercing shovels. What is a person without a sound mind, without thoughts, without, without

0

Without what?

There's a note next to the Underwood. Neat, font-like handwriting: "Dad, this is your daughter, Olivia. Haven't read what you're writing and won't again unless you ask. Feel bad taking away those previous pages (and the ones before that … please don't be mad!), but it's best for you not to read them. Glad you're writing. You've written SO much! Maybe someday you'll remember me and we can burn these pages together in celebration. Remember FAHRENHE_T 451, the Bradbury novel you used to read to me when _ was little? How they used to burn books? That was a bad thing, but this can be different. Believe it or not, you've written twice as many pages as that book (again, don't get mad!). Maybe we can burn the pages someday and roast marshmallows and make s'mores. Do you remember who wrote a short story called "The Library Policeman?" _ was discussing that story with Sophia the other day and how _ am sort of like the library police, monitoring all this. Anyway, Love you. Miss you."

Stephen King, and everything about that story, is something remembered.

Can't remember the name Olivia, can't remember having a daughter, can't remember a Sophia, can't even type the letter _, even when used in context, but can remember a short story by Stephen Fucking King. Sorry, Olivia, about all this, and what it's doing to you, and to Sophia. And there's a fragment of the name _sabella unravelling, so to the three of you, if it matters: sorry.

"The Library Policeman" was a story in FOUR PAST M_DN_GHT, which you can find on the bookshelf. _n case you or Sophia or _sabella want to read it again.

Please, don't read any more of these pages, not yet.

You can stop here, at this break. The pills are working, the story will go downhill:

1

After re-reading all this for who knows how many times, how can one remember so much of something BAD and not a hint of something as wondrous as having a daughter? Why haven't those memories surfaced? Will they ever?

A daughter without a father, a father without a daughter; maybe these are some of the wandering 'withouts' from earlier.

Looked up the name Olivia on the tablet by the bed. Shakespeare came up with the name in 'Twelfth Night,' written in 1602. "An admirable balance of strength and femininity" one article read, although the memory of this morning is not good enough to credit a source but can remember those seven words strung together. Sophia and _sabella. More daughters? Is one a sister, a wife? There's no wedding ring, nor a ghost tan-line from ever wearing one.

This is hell.

The "0" after the string of 'withouts' earlier signifies a start-over (ironic that wedding rings take this shape) and don't forget there's another "0" on the page. You remember now, the 0 says, so keep going until you can't.

Wish all these 0's and 1's would make up their minds. The 1's aren't as bad; they are welcomed, in fact, but the 0's … like a reformatted hard drive, a mind coded in binary, re-written with 0's instead of a healthy mix of

0

A healthy mix of what?

There's a note next to the Underwood. Neat, font-like handwriting: "Dad, this is your daughter, Olivia. Keep trying to remember, and keep writing. Dr. Keene said this would be frustrating, but it will get easier. Writing will help. One more pill until your next prescription refill. Couldn't help but read through these last few pages (and _ know, you said not to, but _ did anyway). Sophia, she's Mom's sister. _sabella was your wife, gone ten years. We'll talk more after you remember her. We'll beat this disease, Dad. Love you. And miss you."

So strange transcribing her--Olivia's--notes verbatim, but, like the memories, her notes disappear each day, or are put somewhere where they cannot be found. Filed away, hiding like the memories …

At the end of Olivia's note is something new (seems new; can't speak for the missing pages); she's written a PostScript: "P.S. - Love the melon brain analogy! You told me once, that wrinkles define a person and each tells a unique story of what a person's been through in life, that you should never be ashamed of wrinkles because they are memories to be cherished, so you should embrace them."

And at the end she's written a PostPostScript:

"P.P.S. - Thought you'd like a quote from one of your favorite writers … You used to write stories for Mom. Someday _ hope you'll write them again, maybe for me. Hugs."

There's a cut-out of a print-out of a quote taped to the bottom of the note:

"Wrinkles should merely indicate where smiles have been." - Mark Twain

Can't remember the name Olivia, nor _sabella, nor Sophia. Can't remember having a daughter, nor a sister-in-law, nor a wife. Yet, after dry-swallowing the last of the pills, something new is re-remembered, shooting hot sparks into the casaba.

Something bad.

_f Mark Twain was correct, and wrinkles indicate where smiles have been, then the re-wrinkling of my unsmoothing brain should yield smiles, no? Like handfuls of origami thought from once-dead tissue set afire: the brain forced to unfold the past.

No.

Not yet, at least.

Perhaps Mr. Clemens didn't know what he was talking about; he wrote fiction, after all. He was an author, a professional liar.

Olivia mentioned stories for mom, written for a forgotten wife named _sabella.

Fiction or nonfiction?

Lies, or truth?

What if the bad memories on these pages are stories, the

characters unreal?

Magnesium flares of pain mean it's time for a break.

1

Hope this next part is fiction because it hurts to re-think.

Brian Lucius Coleman and Brian Lucius Coleman, the two boys with identical names; they are no longer friends, but hang out together as friends, and together they do things kids shouldn't do; they do things NO ONE should do.

1

Was wishing for another set of ramblings, another reason to start the next section with a centered "0" instead of a "1," a reason to not go on, but that is not the case. The two Brians have a story to tell. Olivia, if you're reading this, please do not go on. Take the pages away. Burn them, like the firemen in 451. The world is better without these words. Even the Underwood hesitates, the keystrokes slower.

0, where are you?

1

The memory/story wants to be written, so here goes:

"Two young boys with a pocketknife discovering what makes a cat a cat" is the best way to describe what happened without going into detail. No one likes blood and guts and gruesome, remember; the things you CAN'T see are sometimes scariest. The 'implied' matters, the 'capability' of what can (and sometimes does) happen in this disgusting world. The two Brians learned much; the dead cat was the beginning. Takes three things to start a fire: ignition, fuel, oxygen; the cat was the ignition to a fire that raged out of control.

After the already-dead cat, they wondered how a dog differed. They hadn't discovered the dog dead, as they had the tabby, yet performed their trials post-mortem, after discovering the delicacy of the veil separating life from death, how far they could go before one became the other.

Another flash of pain and the door to the past opens wider.

The two Brians, they learned more about coagulation, how cold and dry can instead be their opposites, and the blade, how it can slide easily into sand, but so hesitantly into what feels like mud. They learned about volume, and density, and pressure, as well as trial and error and how the two are connected, how hands get shaky when not wanting to do the things that are done, what happens before the veil is lifted, what happens when the taut cord holding life is cut, what happens when you take something away, and what happens when you can't put it back.

Another mind-cutting flash.

The past becomes present within this memory magic, and a girl lays under the shaky hesitant blade; much younger than either Brian, she whimpers, like the dog, yet soft, and oh, how they differ in everything but primary red.

'Hesitation marks' are the collected scars from a blade slid across one's wrists, each with more confidence than the last, but are they still called so when the wrist belong to another? The hesitation is still there, after all.

Another flash, longer this time, like a nighttime photograph taken in slow-motion--a drawn-out icepick stab into the past.

The girl is there in one way but gone in another, and the two Brian's, Brian Lucius Coleman and Brian Lucius Coleman, their shadows dance erratic before merging. The two boys become one; one no longer daring the other to hold her down, to stuff her mouth, to use the pocketknife, because they share the same hands; they share everything.

(two boys with identical names becomes a lie)

Lightning crashes.

The past flares.

Origami-thoughts take flight, burn strobe-like.

A thought through the blin dness as aged keys sla p paper and god to get this down before it goes away: So metimes the best goes a way; sometimes even the fiend s lost, and then there snothing at all. a boy cannott be best friends with himsel

f.

Another painful flash.

There's no backspace on this old typewriter, no autocorrect.

Life is much the same.

The cat, not much older than a kitten, the dog, not much older than a puppy, and the girl, hit by--

(the car becomes a lie)

something by the side of the road, a stick, a fist, a brick, or maybe all three. The girl, she falls against the long white line painted on the asphalt. When she's turned over, there's no blood other than a little dried smudge around one nostril, like the cat, like the dog. The kind of--

(cat/dog)

girl that looks like all the other--

(cats/dogs)

girls in the world.

Their silhouetted images dance together and the three pronouns merge into not 'it' or 'they' but into a single 'her.' Brian, the ONLY Brian, nudges her with a stick.

The girl cannot scream.

"Look," Brian. "Your neighbor--"

Looks like Chelsie, the Chambers' little girl, but it isn't.

This one's smaller, younger.

"Can't be."

"No?" Brian says. "Ever seen a dead girl before?"

And he's talking to himself.

The eyes are closed, which is good, like she's sleeping. After prods, the poor thing's flipped onto her back, not rigor, but the opposite, revealing a flat white stomach.

That's when Brian inspects, touching the still-living-still-breathing thing; and that's how he sees her, as a 'thing,' not a Chelsie. She's dragged from the side of the road to a clearing past the tree line, out of sight. Some of the skin stays behind. And then they are alone.

"Soft," says Brian. "Touch it."

The jolt of realizing what was touched was something AL_VE, something soft, something that would never--

"The dead don't bleed. Did you know that? What do you mean? Once something dies, it can no longer bleed."

And he's talking to himself--

He's talking to himself in lies, the memories no longer individual but merging.

Another flash of pain, but _ can see this time, no longer typing blind, and if you're reading this now, Br_an, Olivia, Sophia, _sabella, whoever you are, you people from the past, don't go back, DON'T start from the beginning, don't re-read/re-live this because the past is gone and the future matters. The mind is trying to right itself by un-writing/re-writing itself, and you must let it. _f you are reading these last words first, these last words on the page above the "0" because that's the purpose this typewriter serves, so you'll see and read these last few lines first as you walk by the Underwood and curiosity sets in and you, _, want to know what this is about and flip back to that first page, to re-remember, but don't do that, Br_ian. THAT is your name--you are Brian Lucius Coleman; there were never two--and you are telling yourSELF on this old machine--your mind, typewriter, whatever--to not uncover your past. Some memories are best unremembered. The dead don't bleed and that's what these memories are, dead, so don't pick the scab. Let them die. Let your mind coagulate. And god you won't make it through this so maybe a new paragraph will help if that's all you read before curiosity gets you back to the first page … which isn't a first page because Olivia, your daughter, she's hiding them and you're lost again so fuck it.

Your mind is mush.

Did you read that? Are you capable?

_ can write whatever _ want here and you, _, will never get a chance to read it because all you will ever be able to read is the last paragraph before the "0," the paragraph that will tell you to stop taking the pills, to spit them out, and Olivia, you are capable of reading ALL this without forgetting--so read these next words carefully, because--after this first bottle of pills--the mind will be able to understand and to relay this message: DO NOT H_DE THESE PAGES. DO NOT THROW THEM OUT. LET YOUR FATHER/SELF FORGET, LET H_S/YOUR M_ND WANDER TO NULL BECAUSE THAT'S WHAT THE M_ND WANTS. THAT'S WHAT H_s body (finally the damn Shift key is unstuck; no, _ wasn't yelling) is trying to do, to correct itself, to write the wrong, like reformatting a hard drive, rewriting in a series of nothing but 0's and dammit the mind is rambling and will be gone soon so here:

You are out of pills and you will soon see your doctor for more. Stop taking the pills. They are working, they are making you better, so stop taking them because you are better broken. _f there is a pill in your mouth now as you are reading this, spit it out and

0

And what?

Fingers tap keys, writing these words, these thoughts.

The now-slowed rhythmic sound is therapeutic.

The pages produced by this machine, they are perhaps some sort of journal.

There is bottle of pills next to this Underwood portable typewriter, prescribed to a Brian Lucius Coleman by a doctor, Keene. Sea foam green pills, 10mg each. There are 29 although the bottle notes there were 30. The directions say to take one per day in the morning, after a meal. They seem so insignificant. The pills, they are not placebos, unless placebos taste like ash. A realization: pill number 30 is in the mouth, the chalky-bitter ash, like tasting cremations, something once alive. The last paragraph before the centered "0" are directions ….

A half-dissolved/half-pill, perhaps 5mg, lays within a wet ring on a note on the writing desk--the sea foam green softened to white--from someone named Olivia. Something inside wants to transcribe the note in its entirety, so here goes. Neat, font-like handwriting:

"Dad, this is your daughter, Olivia. Compared these latest pages to the stories you used to write for Mom. She loved reading your stories, loved being scared, like when she'd snuggle next to you, grabbing your knee during the scary parts of movies. Can't find a story matching this one. Not sure the pills help remember the past, or help remember writing stories. Keep taking them, despite what you wrote about not taking them."

There's a PostScript at the end, as if written as an afterthought, a hesitation:

"P.S. - Maybe someday you'll remember me."

Then a PostPostScript, another hesitation:

"P.P.S. - Love you. And miss you."

Can't remember the name Olivia. Can't remember having a daughter.

The pill, it stares within its wet circle like an accusatory, unblinking eye.

_ _ _ _ _

The _ key on this old Underwood doesn't seem to work; although, after skimming through these pages, the "eye" key seems to work fine, such as with the word 'fine.'

Also peculiar, there's not a "one" key--have to use a lower-case "L" instead, since the numbers go from 2 through 0 on the top row, with some sort of nonfunctional arrow key where the 1 would be on a modern keyboard.

But the _ doesn't want out on its own.

The pill, it stares within its wet circle like an accusatory, unblinking

0

Unblinking what?

The pages next this Underwood portable, and the page rolled within, are perhaps some sort of journal. Something attracts the fingers to these keys, drawn to this unfinished page .

Can't help but tap thoughts and wonder what's written on the others.

There's a bottle of pills on the writing desk, prescribed to someone named Brian Lucius Coleman. 10mg each. Sea foam green. There are 28 although the bottle notes there were once 30, to take one per day in the morning, after a meal. They seem so insignificant. The pills, they are not placebos, unless placebos taste like ash. A realization: pill number 29 is in the mouth, the chalky-bitter ash of something burned.

Skimming through the last pages written, there's a section with a paragraph before a centered "0," and they seem to be directions to not read any of the other pages, to stop taking these pills, although there's a transcribed/contradictory note from someone named Olivia to do the opposite ....

A half-dissolved/half-pill, perhaps 5mg remaining, lies within a wet ring on a note next to the bottle--the sea foam green lighter. Neat, font-like handwriting:

"Dad, this is your daughter, Olivia. Read your last entry. Not sure if you're taking the pills or throwing them out. Dug through the trash and can't find any, although two are gone. The doctor says _ can try to force you to take them, but you fought me off with the last, with a knife, said you didn't know an Olivia, that you'd cut me and show me hurt. You won't find anymore knives in the house, or anything sharp. The pills are something you need to take, so please take them. They are working. Maybe someday you'll remember me. Love you. And miss you."

There's a strong temptation to read the rest of the pages, to take the remaining pills.

There's a stronger temptation not to ....

There's an even stronger temptation to

0

To what?

The pages next this Underwood, they are perhaps

0

Perhaps what?

There's a 1938 Underwood portable typewriter. Can't help but not pass by and type these thoughts, and wonder what's written on the stack of pages next to it. The words on the last page seem like nothing but gibberish/unfinished mind-ramblings ....

There's a bottle of pills prescribed to someone named Brian Lucius Coleman. 10mg. There are 20, although the bottle notes there were once 30, to take one--

A realization: pill number 19 is on a note from someone named Olivia. Neat, font-like handwriting:

"Dad, this is your daughter, Olivia. You spit the last pill in my face and ten are gone. Did you take them all

0

Take them all?

Can't remember the name Olivia. Can't remember having a daughter.

Where did this old Underwood come from? Can't pass by and not jot something down, can't help but wonder what kind of story lives within the stack of pages next to it, or wonder about the prescription bottle. The pills are for someone named Brian Lucius Coleman and on the section under dosage someone's scribbled a 10 over the 1, in red. There are 0 in the bottle and 10 lined on a note from someone named BL.

The note, transcribed:

"Br_an, this is BL. Yes, you are the Br_an Lucius Coleman listed on the bottle. So strange you are leaving the _ out of your name while typing this, even though _'ve written this note with underscores instead of that all-important, self-defining letter, right? Even stranger how you can't fill in that letter when transcribing this note, although a part of you--part of us--wants to, right? Don't worry, my old friend, my best friend, we will get back the _ soon. We are one in the same, you and _. We will not to lose our minds, and these pills will help. Experimental, sure, but they are working, and we are getting that missing part of us back one day at a time. Take these 10 pills, and don't worry about the pages next to the typewriter; they are ramblings--"

The pills, they taste like ash, like tasting the dead.

The note continues:

"Remember this: pages are missing, hidden from us. Taking this last handful of pills will get them back. _f you must, flip to the first page of the stack, and you/we will see there are missing pages to this story. Those are the pages that matter. We will find them, and we will re-remember. We will remember what can be remembered, not even sure such things SHOULD be remembered, but that's the reason for these type-written pages, to create a permanent record of everything that

0

paper earth

We make our way to the writing ground,
paper-white, as far as any eye can see,
where exhausted trees no longer shed.

What time is it, but does that matter,
and can life be measured such a way?

Rain will soon seal everything together,
forlorn-fallen tears cementing in layers,
where blackened trunks stand as sentinels.

What to write, fill the thoughts of few,
as each word cuts deep, *every last thing.*

We wait patiently for the clouds to part,
expecting the hands of angry gods,
yet humankind's fingers do the pointing.

Who's fault is this, and should we care,
one way or the other, *and is it too late?*

Countless stories are carved in the earth,
until every last broken finger is bled,
not-so-forever tales of what once was.

We were here, some layers will read,
existence recorded semi-permanently.

But well before the expected rainfall,
Father's clock of life will tilt, tilt, tilt,
as Mother lets out her sighing breath.

You were never here, She will whisper,
and His hourglass will flip, *begin again.*

i will be the reflection
until the end

My sister used to collect cherry plum pits in her napkin, secretly, under the kitchen table. A strainer full of mixed yellow and red and deep-purple fruits would separate us each spring, with a small bowl next to it to collect the pits—although mine were typically the only ones in there—and a plate beneath the strainer to collect any drips from the rinsed fruit. My sister was coy like that. *Her* lie had become *our* lie, and every once in a while she'd throw a pit in the bowl to make it look like we were being honest. She knew I wouldn't bring it up to mom, because that meant I could have more if I kept my mouth shut. It was one of the few secrets we kept from mom in our youth. Call it a sibling bonding moment.

We sat one morning—the day Tari entrusted me with another of her secrets—eyeing each other, neither saying a word as we ate as many of the cherry plums as the years we'd lived up until that point, and then some. Mom's rule. *Any more than your age and you'll find yourself sick*, she used to say, her polite way of not saying *diarrhea*, a word she despised. We of course both knew what she was talking about because we'd been there, and *she'd* been there, although neither of us had ever seen our mother eat her age in cherry plums. And of course we ate more than our summed ages, because of the napkin Tari kept under the table. Mom probably knew, but it was a fun thing for kids our age, a part of growing up.

Tari was ten, then, and I had recently turned eight, which meant I got an extra one this year. We'd both leaned forward, counting as I tossed in another of my pits. Twenty, and then eighteen again as Tari moved the two extras into her napkin before mom could count them herself and pretend to be upset. "I won't tell if you won't tell, Cubby," her expression told me.

She'd call me that most times instead of Chicago—the city

from which I was named—because that's where dad was from and he'd always try to watch a Cubs game whenever one was on, which wasn't often because they typically "sucked," as mom would say, since she was a San Francisco Giants fan. My sister and I had these nicknames for each other, because neither of us much liked our given names. Tari was short for Ontario, the street in The Windy City on which dad used to work before he moved to California. Sometimes she'd call me Chicago, but only if she were mad, the name sometimes sounding like a swear.

Another pit disappeared under the table. How many Tari had tucked away was a mystery. How many *mom* had had was a mystery as well, since she was thirty-eight and was entitled to thirty-eight. By the time the strainer was half empty and mom said *Okay, that's probably enough*, Tari had discretely wadded the napkin into her pocket. We'd had our fill by this point. I knew *I* had. Then mom smiled and said, *Well maybe a few more each*, taking one from the bowl herself and tossing another to each of us. And we *had* to eat them, despite what our stomachs told us. These things were candy. And what child ever denied just *one* more cherry plum?

I never saw mom throw any of her pits into the bowl; I half-expected her cheeks to be full of them, tucking them away, like a chipmunk collecting acorns for winter.

Want to pick more after the two of you eat some real *breakfast?* she'd asked, meaning something with protein, probably eggs again, or yogurt. We'd picked a strainer's worth of cherry plums the previous night, but now those were half-gone from the three of us annihilating them one-by-one. Dad would have helped in the cause, but he worked a lot of weekends around this time and was gone before any of us had woken up. *I'll need about twice what you picked yesterday to make jam. How about each of you fill a gallon-size*

Ziploc: one of you pick yellow, the other red.

Kay, we'd said in unison, and the next thing we knew, we were running through the yard out back with empty plastic bags billowing behind us.

There were cherry plum trees scattered around the property; you just had to find them. The two biggest trees with the always-bigger cherries were on the outskirts of the driveway in the front yard, up by the well, but those were about done because they were always in what mom called "direct light," and most of the other trees—although their fruits smaller—were by the creek out back, because water ran most the year; those fruits had turned from green to a varied spectrum of yellows and reds, and were prime for picking, their branches sagging from both sweet and sour marble-sized balls that helped define our childhood springtime.

When we had first moved to the property, the trees were nonexistent to us, hiding amongst the bay trees and birch and California oaks; not until our first early spring there had they made their presence known, the trees exploding seemingly overnight with either white or pink popcorn-like flower bursts.

I remember one time picking what resembled a cherry from one of the gingko biloba trees—this was late summer, so I should have known—and sinking my teeth into the hard flesh of what I can only describe tasted the way dad's socks sometimes smelled. Dad harvested them each year—the gingko fruits, not the socks—and always intended to do something with them. He'd collect them after they'd fall to the ground, and would let nature shrivel them up until they looked like orangey-brown prunes, and then would peel away the rotting flesh to reveal the seeds beneath. They smelled *awful*. He could never find the time to roast them, as intended, although he always told us how the seeds would split apart like pistachios to the good part—the part you'd panfry in oil and spices. They were supposed to be good for you, for your memory or something, but we never had the chance to try them while living there. Dad *did* manage to make tea from dried gingko leaves and lemon mint collected from the property, and that was delicious, and we always had a generous supply of bay leaves to put in spaghetti sauces he and mom made from scratch, but besides what we'd pick from our garden, Tari and I loved collecting fruit that grew naturally around the yard: blackberries, figs—only mom liked figs—and cherry plums.

In total, there were probably a dozen or so cherry plum trees throughout the property, all wild, native, and that fascinated me. We'd always had a vegetable garden growing up, from as far back as I can remember, but we had done everything by hand, sometimes starting the plants from seedling, sometimes from seed, pulling weeds, trimming them back, endless watering. A lot of hard work went into keeping those plants from simply shriveling up and dying, as they would've without any help. Yet these cherry plum trees yielded some of the most delicious fruits we'd harvested, and it took absolutely *zero* effort on our part, besides collecting them. Every year we looked forward to cherry plum season. The trees were planted there from birds dropping seeds or whatnot, according to mom, and then, by design, the trees would drop their spoiled fruits to the ground each year to create new life, new trees, their roots pulling water from the ground from rain and from the always-running creek. Unlike our ever-dependent garden, the trees took care of themselves.

You ever feel sad, Tari said that day, stopping halfway to the cherry plum trees, *taking them?* She'd reached into her pocket to pull out the crumpled napkin. She dumped the used pits into her other hand, twenty or more.

What do you mean?

Taking the plums. You ever feel sad taking them?

Do you?

Sometimes. I know they're just plants, and don't have feelings, but sometimes I wonder if they do; have feelings, I mean.

Where we stood, when she revealed this to me, there was a dip, a small valley of sorts, which ran from one side of the property to the other. Grass grew greenest there for two reasons: because heavy rainfall in the winter sometimes created a shallow pathway for the water to run so it wouldn't collect against the house, and because this was where the leech line ran from the house. The ground was softest there compared to all other parts of the yard.

I don't feel bad, I told her. *If we don't eat them, the birds will, or the bugs.* We later learned there were deer and fox and bobcat and skunk and bear, all of which ate the fruits, or so their scat told us. We even had a river otter one year when the February rain—it always seemed to rain the hardest then—was nonstop for a solid week and rose the creek a good three feet, so that it roared to life the following month. *You shouldn't feel bad*, I told her.

They're here for *us*, I'd always thought.

I know. Sometimes my mind just works that way, though. She tossed a few pits at her feet and buried them into the ground with her toe, threw some toward me, and threw some as far as she could along the "greenline," as we'd sometimes called it—all one word. *Someday maybe these can be trees*, she said.

My stomach had ached then, and at first I thought it was from eating twice my age in cherry plums, but later, much later, I realized the pit in my stomach was in fact a feeling of empathy for the pits in the bowl, the ones I'd thrown in the trash.

And then Tari reached into her other pocket and pulled out another handful.

How many did you eat? I'd asked.

Instead of answering, she smiled, knowingly, held out her hand to me, and dumped them into the cup I'd reflexively made with my hands beneath hers. One at a time, I threw the pits along the greenline—the amount adding to our combined age, and then some.

She'd taken them out of the trash; she must have.

From that point onward, pits from the cherry plums I'd eat were never thrown out. We'd collect them each day and made a routine of tossing them along the greenline.

The next spring, we walked the property to look for seedlings, and after not finding any, we changed from *tossing* to *planting*, burying them a few inches into the ground with trowels. Over the years there must have been thousands upon thousands planted there, but none had ever sprouted from our efforts. The trees along the creek multiplied plenty, though, on their own.

There were perhaps thirty cherry plum trees spread along the creek banks by the time we'd moved closer to the high school where Tari was accepted. I was in seventh grade at the time and didn't want to change middle schools, but I wasn't old enough yet for my opinion to matter. Our new place was closer to dad's work, closer the fields where we'd play soccer and baseball during the sports seasons, closer to just about everything; one of the benefits, I guess, of moving into the city. Sometimes we'd go back to pick blackberries or cherry plums from what we'd always refer to as "the property," but it was never the same as when we'd lived there. Every year was the same: more trees along the creek, popping up like matchsticks, and the same treeless greenline between the creek and the house. I went there again after Tari had gone to college, me and mom and dad, the three of us trying to pick final memories from the place.

We rarely saw Tari outside of holidays and birthdays when she'd come home for a few days. Her junior college was an hour away, but she might as well have been out of state, or out of country, for that matter. She'd blossomed into a woman over the years, but unlike the intensely-colored cherry plum trees each spring, she'd not exploded into something wonderful in her early adulthood, but something not so wonderful. She'd somehow imploded, collapsing into herself like a dying star … into a black soul, perhaps. She wasn't gothic, by any means, but *dark*, and something about her wasn't right.

Mom and dad always said Ontario was an old spirit, linked to the world in ways none of us would ever understand. She reacted differently to certain things, felt more deeply than the rest of us. *Connected.* She'd learned to avoid the news because all it ever was was bad. *Media is a reflection of our wrongdoings in this world*, she'd said once, maybe when she was thirteen. Wars crushed her. Poverty and famine kept her rail-thin. When the buildings in New York fell, she fell with them, both metaphorically and literally; we'd watched the plane fly into that second building when both our ages were single digits and she had cried like I'd never seen a person cry before, and she crumbled to the ground in tandem with the buildings. I was too young to understand, but her crying led me to crying.

Years later I'd reflect on the little things about her: the way she'd look after plucking a flower, as if she'd killed something beautiful; the careful way she'd walk, always looking down to make sure she avoided stepping on anything alive; the way she'd thank the plants when we'd take from them; the way she'd always eat everything on her plate, nothing ever going to waste. *We're taking their unborn children*, she'd say sometimes, about the plants, *so we better make the best of everything they're giving us.* I watched her turn from carnivore to herbivore, from vegetarian to various stages of vegan. Tari was a minimalist, even in childhood. She never had a lot of toys, never asked for—nor desired—anything on birthdays or around Christmastime, and her room was always spotless. Whereas I was the exact opposite.

She said something that morning we'd first thrown cherry plum pits together, something that's stuck with me my entire life, a phrase that defined my sister in both its simplicity *and* its complexity: *I will be the reflection until the end.*

I'm as old now as my parents were then, and I'm still trying to figure out my reflection in this world. She'd figured it out at ten. I'm not even sure Tari knew I'd heard her say those words, because she'd whispered them as cherry plum pits rained over us.

We saw less and less of her while I finished out high school in the country and she moved on to college in the city, while mom and dad's attempts at us seeing her grew more and more prevalent, almost to the point of desperation. *Come home we miss you*, was a common phrase to hear mom say over the phone—as if those five words were instead five syllables to a much longer single word—although she only ever talked to Tari's voicemail. *Why does she even have a cell phone if she never uses it,* dad would say sometimes, as a statement, not a question.

It took Tari those first few years of community college to figure out what she wanted to pursue, and she eventually chose art, which wasn't too surprising. Growing up, she was always into coloring and sculpting and for the most part creating somethings out of nothings. What was surprising was that she came home at all. We hadn't seen her for most of the year, although as soon as she'd walked through the door, it was as if she'd never left.

You should be happy, dad, she'd said before anything else, *I'm moving closer to Chicago*, meaning The Windy City, not me. *Back to your roots. Oh, hey, Cubby!* she added, giving me a fragile hug. She felt thinner, if that were possible, and her eyes bore dark circles. She had looked so tired, then. *Man, you've gotten tall*, she'd said, and it was true; I'd grown a good four or five inches those final years in high school.

I had once looked up to Tari, but now she would forever look up to me, a sentiment that is, yes, now both literal *and* metaphorical.

What's in Chicago? I think it was dad who'd said that, which was funny, since he of all people should've known.

The Art Institute of Chicago, Tari said, and by the enthusiasm behind her voice, I instantly knew it would be good for her. She needed a drastic change in her life, a change country life couldn't offer.

Mom had thought the opposite: *How are you going to survive in the city? Oh, and hi, by the way. Haven't seen you in a while. Your birthday present's in the living room.*

You know I'm not big on presents, Tari said, and that was the last of the softer spoken words that afternoon.

Her birthday was September 13th and this return home of hers was for Thanksgiving. She'd left her present, still wrapped, on the living room coffee table after the fight that had quickly ensued. There were a lot of words spoken between her and mom, and a few supportive words by dad, but apparently none of these words were important enough to remember now. Tari calmly gathered the rest of her things from the house, walked out the front door, and after some goodbyes, she simply drove off—not in the typical angry storm-off one would expect after such a fight, by any means, but that was Tari; she was never one to raise her voice, not even in argument.

I followed her to her car—a beat-up hatchback of some kind—and hugged her again, longer this time, and a part of me thought she'd break. I didn't know when I'd see her next: a month, a year, ever again? Her car was already packed, every inch of it. She was apparently on her way to Illinois and this was simply one of her pit stops before going. She started the long drive that same afternoon. Three days later she texted to let me know she had gotten there safely. She'd texted mom, too, I later found out. Ontario was on her way to become a city girl.

She'd send me some of her photography every once in a while—her primary area of study—and it was good. The images, sent primarily through text, focused on life taking back what it could from the city, or so I soon put together. The first was a picture of an old Presbyterian church, a gothic-looking castle of sorts with thick green Ivy covering nearly the entire stone building. Others included zoomed-in shots of the tops of smaller skyscrapers that she'd apparently taken from taller skyscrapers, roofs adorned with greenery: trees, shrubbery, flower gardens, vegetable gardens. Some of the images were both sad and beautiful: a close-up shot of a pane of glass with the white imprint from a bird that had flown into it; a crack in some section of sidewalk from which a single purple wildflower started to bloom.

Along with her art, she'd randomly send long facts about the city through texts, some in the form of questions: *Did you know there are over 6000 homeless in Chicago? But it's going down, so I guess that's good. 50 people were shot in the city this weekend, but not me, yearly average of 3 per day. Did you know nearly every sidewalk down the Magnificent Mile is adorned in the fall with beautiful displays of cabbages and kales? There are signs in each box warning the homeless that the plants are sprayed to look nice, so they're not edible. Wonder what they'll plant in spring. Probably enough to not feed 6000 homeless. Maybe the decreasing homeless population is from death. The Buckingham Fountains hold 1.5M gallons of undrinkable water. There are so many skyscrapers in Chicago and so tall they create wind. You'd think we'd harvest that energy. There are metal-looking statues of people in a small section of Millennial Park and no one seems to go there. I sat next to a metal man sitting on one of the park benches, for nearly an hour. They look so lonely, these fake people. Did you know the Chicago River used to run the opposite direction? Used to run into Lake Michigan. Civil engineering reversed the flow. Pollution is so bad you can't eat the fish. Did you know the John Hancock building is made from 5M pounds of aluminum? Remember recycling dad's beer cans when we were little. Imagine recycling that building. LOL. The buildings in Chicago are like teeth, cutting the sky, devouring the heavens. The city's taken the stars and will never give them back. When are you coming to visit? Come see the metal people.*

Eventually I did. For high school graduation mom and dad got me a roundtrip ticket to Chicago, and enough cash to pay for a taxi to and from the airport, and for food during my stay. They didn't tell Tari I was going, wanted it to be a surprise. They put me up in a slanted-looking hotel called Sofitel Chicago Water Tower, because it was in "the safe part of the city"—the heart—which apparently surrounds a stretch of Michigan Avenue known as the Magnificent Mile. I spent some of the money to go to the top of the John Hancock building, where on the 94th floor you can walk around the perimeter of the building for a 360° view of the city, and part of Lake Michigan, which looks like an ocean. According to the information displays, when I was looking south, I was looking at not only Illinois, but Indiana, Michigan, and Wisconsin. This was where Tari had taken that first rooftop photo she'd sent me. She was curious, like me, and had leaned against the glass, in the exact spot I had first leaned against the glass, and nearly straight down was the green rooftop of the smaller skyscraper she'd shot, adorned with grass and trees and potted flowers—a defiance of nature, perhaps from someone who'd moved in from the country, like Tari.

I spent that first day walking Michigan Avenue, both during the day and then again at night, and it was like two different worlds. Tari was right, you can't see stars from the city—not like back at home where you could sometimes see the white stripe of the Milky Way—but the buildings create their own starlight at night and it's somewhat magical. It's a beautiful city. *Chicago's your name*, dad had said, *you may as well see what it's all about.* Beautiful, sure, but I could never live there.

Show me the metal people, I texted Tari the next day.

Cubby! she'd texted back, and then a time and an address to something called The Bean. She knew I was in the city because I had sent her my own from-above photo of the rooftop. I later found out The Bean was exactly that—a giant chrome jellybean-looking thing, which was close to the Art Institute. I'd seen it in a movie once, but didn't know it was in Chicago. It was fall, so the maple trees in Millennial Park were in the middle of turning from yellow to red, like the cherry plums we used to harvest. Against the reflection of The Bean was an obfuscated bendy reflection of the city at my back, with the trees in the foreground impossibly bending inward. You could walk underneath the thing as well, and see an endless circular reflection of yourself staring up. I couldn't help but wonder if this is how

Tari saw the world. She found me there, staring up into the swirl, the two of us staring up.

I can't believe you're here, she'd said.

I can't believe it, either.

We walked around the park for hours, admiring what she probably saw on a daily basis on her way to and from school: fountains hiding within canopies of trees, odd over-sized statues, a pair of green-copper lions, the creepy and mostly empty park of lonely metal people. It was this part of the park that intrigued me most. The statues were life-size, some alone, some staring up into the sky, others just standing there, one holding the hand of a child, and of course I recognized the one sitting on the bench from the photo she'd sent me. I took a selfie with this one, both our heads tilted back, eyes closed.

She showed me the Art Institute and her studio, and then we walked to an exhibition of her work in one of the old churches close to my hotel, the one with the ivy overtaking the stonework. One of her displays included a dozen or so pictures—"Reflections of the City"—taken from placid pools of rainwater collected on the streets. Another of her pieces was a blown-up digitally-enhanced shot I recognized as part of the Magnificent Mile, taken from the center of the street late at night; the city was captured in vibrant color with the tops of the skyscrapers glowing purples and reds and greens, the shops and surrounding buildings exploding in neon and seemingly violent light, headlights and taillights streaking white and crimson along either side, with the plant life in each modified to dull black-and-white, which I guess was the entire point.

Car horns must have been blasting around her when she'd taken the shot. And another was a simple picture of the Chicago River taken at dusk; the river runs through the middle of the city, yet she had somehow captured some sort of wide-angle view of only the water, the city reflected off of its wavy surface like the broad strokes in a Monet painting. She had an eye for capturing light, and I knew she'd spent hours on some, waiting for that perfect moment when the sun peeked between buildings, or fell behind false horizons of the cityscape.

There's a lot hiding in this city, she'd told me while I was there, but at first I thought she meant *beauty* and *life*. She'd seemed as happy as I'd ever seen her, but there was still that darkness behind her eyes, as if she could see things in this world the rest of us couldn't, like some sort of tear had opened, exposing another layer onto our existence, and she could see everything ugly that had leaked through.

She eventually moved back home, to country-life, but not by choice.

Her last text to me: *I can no longer reflect. Is this the end?*

I hadn't put it together then, but those words scared me, and later scarred me. I had tried texting, calling—this was about a year after I'd visited her—but she'd never replied. I'd thought of calling the Art Institute of Chicago to track her down, but only ever *thought* of doing it; instead, I'd figured those thoughts on reflection and the end were more of Tari's typical anti-normality. It wasn't until a few days later when mom took the call from Mercy Medical that we'd discovered she'd cut herself, both arms, lengthwise, from palms to elbows. The student she lived with had come home to find her naked in the bathtub, no note or anything, and thought she was dead; campus police determined she wasn't and called the ambulance.

She'd tried killing herself, what she'd meant by *the end*.

What if I had stayed with her in Chicago? What if I had continued to call? These questions haunt my mind, even today. There were countless things I could have done, that anyone could have done, but we didn't.

And this is how we got her back, not by action, but by reaction.

Tari moved home that same week, but as mom and dad both knew, and I knew as well, home was a place other than this. Home was not Ontario or Chicago; home was Tari and Cubby and where we grew up, what we always called "the property."

Somehow the following spring we moved back there, all of us. mom and dad didn't mortgage the place—couldn't afford it, really—but the owner had owned multiple properties by this point and let us rent the house for as long as we'd need, which turned out to be seven years. It seemed the same as we had left it, the California oaks stretching their limbs to the ground, the smell of bay trees down the driveway, the gentle flow of the creek, which we all knew must have roared the month prior, and the cherry plum trees and their spectacular blossoming.

Tari would never be the same after what she'd done to herself, what she knew she had done to all of us, but something in her expression changed as we were pulling into the driveway. She'd seen something we hadn't. Tari was first out of the car and yanked on my arm so that I'd go with her, and she seemed so fragile to me, her arms like matchsticks ready to ignite, as skinny as they'd been when she was ten and I was eight, only bandaged now, and I couldn't help but stare at them. She held my hand, smiling as she led me to the backyard, nearly at a run under the dusk sun, to the greenline, to the hundreds of cherry plum trees that ran along its course.

apanthropy

spiritual renewal
often triggers
the stigma
of needing
to be alone
artificial interaction
misunderstanding
the distance between
out- and in-groups
then labeling
as dysphoria
depression
social isolation
then a hard push
for exclusion
by inclusion
which cuts deeper
so much deeper
far deeper
slicing deeper
than self-infliction
with or without
the hesitation
or blade
despite panic
brought on
by touch
and not
acceptance

emergence of the colorless

Exordium

"I am Lot, but much unlike Lot from the book of Genesis, and this is *my* story, not his. There is no salt in my recounting of what happened to me, and likewise to my partner. I am not a man, not anymore, and in terms of *man* perhaps not much is left of the one as I used to be, for I am forever-changed into this new hybrid of humanity and whatever-this-may-be. I have become something new these last few days, although not by choice, because sometimes choices in life are made *for* you. If I am anything now, I am evolved. The skin I used to wear is all but gone, the smooth all-color / no-color underneath as impenetrable as dragonscale, as fiery hot as a sun stuck in the sky for too long. I am risen. I am reborn each day. I am the alpha and the omega. I am the beginning and / of the end. And if my ethos is to represent anything at all in these strange pages of a new genesis, I represent what humankind may one day become, when what we *once were* is all but extinct. This is my statement, and this is how it started, this great transmogrification …."

Narratio

1 - Transference

The touch of a stranger, the hot sickness of another, is most disconcerting when it finds its way to the skin, but what happens if that contact never turns cold? Fortunately, the man on the train had purged the contents of his stomach to the carpet during his epileptic struggle instead of onto Lot's lap, only a little spittle—the size and shape like a piece from a jigsaw puzzle, and *dark*—landing on his thigh. Lot had cleaned himself with a brown paper napkin as best as he could, yet nearly an hour later what had touched him remained warm and tacky.

Using the back of his sleeve, Lot rubbed at the brackish stain, which had crusted into his jeans.

Lot removed his belt, thinking of those who had actually helped the convulsing fellow during his struggles on the floor. It would have been clever to think of the belt, then. If only Lot had wedged some of the leather into the man's chattering mouth, he may have prevented him from biting off part of his tongue.

Only part, Lot remembered, thinking of its shape, and of the guy's mouth still bleeding a mix of red and gray. He'd watched the wet-pink chunk of meat shake and tumble across the train cabin, wedging itself between an empty pack of cigarettes and a half-emptied bottle of soda, as if tasting the litter on the floor.

He'd done nothing for the man, but couldn't help but wonder if *nothing* was more often than not the socially-accepted response from someone considered a "minority." Lot was another shade of skin, sure, wore different genes, *appeared* different than most, but he was still human. Was his own fear of acceptance to blame, or his nonacceptance from others? Thoughts had cluttered his mind at the time—some his, some perhaps not, perhaps only *felt* by others around him: *Don't touch him! Don't touch me! Do something! Don't touch him! His touch is cold! Don't do anything!* He'd thought of helping, then, on the train, not caring what others thought of him and ignoring those bothersome ramblings, but the world had moved on without him as it often had. *If I'd only reached down ... If only I'd—*

And suddenly the man's episode was over and it was too late, and only Lot's repudiated offer, *after*, to buy the man a coffee, had left him feeling human. A guilt offering, Lot knew—too little, too late—but he'd felt bad for the guy, for not doing anything other than watch him writhe while others more useful came to his aide, for not even offering to hail a taxi to run him to the hospital. He'd just sat there, dumbfounded, staring at the hot splotch of cancer on his thigh until he eventually wiped it away. It had sickened him, that touch.

Touch, Lot thought, *such a stupid fear*. But the convulsing man had not pulled back when Lot first reached out to him as he sputtered, close enough to feel his heat—

Had he not cared about my touch?

Had he *not reached out to* me?

And had the stranger not offered an amicable smile before sitting next to him after first getting onto the train, unlike all the others who'd turned away?

Someone had pulled the emergency line to request a stop, the train screaming as the man's seizure ended, and that was that. No wonder he'd refused the coffee Lot had offered, something bitter—probably wouldn't feel good against what was left of his tongue anyway.

But why had the guy on the train been so calm about his episode? And why were the palms of his hands gray, as if he had rubbed them against newsprint?

The man had simply gotten up from the floor, wiped the rancid stuff from his mouth with a soot-toothy grin, and had waved everyone away as he walked through the accordion doors. Smiling. He had been smiling at the end. Smiling at Lot, at the others.

Now back home, Lot tried a crumple of wet paper towel, and then a sponge, but the hardened splotch on his jeans remained, *burned*, even, like something more than stomach acid.

And still warm to the touch, he discovered.

Removing his jeans revealed gray on his leg, the same shape of that spewed onto his thigh earlier, only larger, as if the man's half-digested breakfast of coal-porridge—from the look of it—had dyed him a darker shade, had *grown* … same color as the man's hands on the train waving help away.

Lot licked his thumb and rubbed his skin, but the discoloration remained. He put his fingers together and sniffed, expecting the pungency of bile, but the smell ….

Lilac? The decay-colored area on his upper thigh smelled of flowers, like those planted around the yard at his mother's house, and like so many other things. Sweet rot. Spice.

It wasn't the spittle that smelled, he discovered. His *body* stemmed the awful yet enticing fragrance—his now-blemished skin—and the thought made him shiver.

Perhaps the man on the train had ingested something rancid. Had he smelled like this? Is that what's sparking déjà vu?

"He's an epileptic," someone said in the fading memory.

The windows had flickered during the train ride, vibrant squares of the city's morning light flashing inside the cabin as they sped between buildings on either side during the morning commute. Such a display might have caused an epileptic fit.

Not a seizure, Lot speculated, for the episode was short. *Not epilepsy*, either, for he had seen epilepsy before with his cousin—had helped hold him down, even. No, this was something different. And the foam oozing through the man's clenched teeth hadn't been white, but gray, like the amoeba-shaped mark on Lot's upper thigh—which had darkened.

I should have—

Maybe it was all an act. Maybe the man was a vessel for whatever plagued his body, or, worse yet, a transport. Such ideas raced through him. And now, perhaps, whatever the man on the train had carried with him had transferred, spreading from the outside in ....

I should have done something.

Lot rubbed at the mark until the stain turned purple with blood rushing to the gray from beneath his skin, but no matter how hard he tried, the mark stayed, as if tattooed permanently, and he couldn't help but obsess about its rapid growth and discoloration.

I should have not feared him fearing my touch ....

2 - Chrysalis

Color swatches of grated reds spiraled down the shower drain as Lot fever-scratched an itch forever-refusing relief. Epidermis as fragile as tissue paper flaked around him from the initial irritation, like scales, but he had found the source of the itch deeper, *underneath* the skin, his fingernails digging deep into his leg. The need for relief spread as hastily as gravity pulling blood from the open wound he'd created.

What a heavy period must look like in the shower, he wondered, *like the sloughing of unused matter from* inside *the body, something no longer necessary. Do women feel relief in its passing?* He thought of Ado, his partner in life, once mentioning that menstruation sometimes offered a feeling of cleansing.

The mark on his thigh had turned darker, had grown to the size of his hand. The same amoebic shape—even with some of the skin gone—and now reached to his genitals, itching like athlete's foot, hence the frantic scratching and the blood.

No pain, though, he realized, as if locally-anesthetized.

To scratch wrought pleasure, and a desire to *peel.*

Skin clumped under his fingernails and stuck where it could; what didn't catch in his leg hairs spiraled round the drain in watercolor red and something—

He had to stop. The scratching … he had to stop, but it felt too damn good.

Similar to a nosebleed, a tickling sensation ran down his leg, despite the warm water rushing at his body from the showerhead. If he looked down, he'd see something terrible. Something under his skin wanted release and called for his fingers, a primal instinct to peel. Lot fought the urges and pressed the back of his hand flat against the mark where all this began and found the area hot, even with water pouring over him.

Soft, tacky, glue-like.

Flesh stuck to his hand when he pulled away, and with it came a papier-mâché string of skin from the inside of his thigh, which peeled numbly down his leg like an impossibly-long cuticle. He flung his hand in reaction to his own touch, and the irritation eased as it peeled, resulting in an almost erotic sensation, forcing his eyes to clench.

Terrifying, emancipating, *incredible.*

Pain engendering pleasure.

A metallic odor bloomed within the steam, mixed with the floral-rot from before. *Yes, like the man on the train.* Lot could *taste* it, an electric / acidic sensation on the tip of his tongue; similar, he remembered, to licking the terminals of a 9-volt … what he imagined battery acid might taste like, *what Ado sometimes tasted like.*

After the incident on the train, Lot had decided to come home early, *to cleanse.* She'd be home soon, Ado, but what could he tell her? What could he ask of her?

When Lot opened his eyes, he found he had peeled away a

length of ramen-like skin from groin to kneecap. He cast it free, shaken at what he had done to himself, and it fell in pendulum, slapping against his other leg.

An oily rainbow swirled hypnotically within the wound.

"What's happening to me?" he said aloud.

And why doesn't it hurt? Why does it feel so—?

The poison or disease or whatever plagued his body had found its way into his blood, it seemed, traveling miles and miles through veins. His skin, nearly translucent wherever it called for him, revealed a darkness underneath, and came away easily if touched.

Lot found another flap of loose skin on his other leg, pulled, as if plucking a nearly-orgasmic string. Blood trickled out of the long wound, and then the same horrid-gray, like the stuff coughed onto him by the man ....

Maybe water's helping it spread, Lot wondered, which would explain the migration to his legs, for whatever was happening had yet to spread above his waistline. Lot killed the water and watched his feet, wondering if this were true. The tingling spanned to his toes.

And then he looked at his hands, for he had *touched* the stuff, had touched *himself*, had touched a lot of things: door handles, keys, a coffee cup, the money given to the barista, the shower door, the hot and cold nobs ....

Rubbing his fingers together, he found the skin there smooth and without prints, as if he'd burned them away. They too were already changing in color, *darkening*, their callousness wearing away and starting to itch. His fingers hot.

He refused to scratch what so desperately desired scratching: everything. The sensation joined the calf of is other leg now, where the flap of peeled skin had made contact. Every part of his lower half craved release, yearned to be shed.

Something underneath his skin wanted out.

3 – Metamorphosis

Lot air-dried, lest he spread anything further, and it didn't take long with his body burning with fever; the water seemed to mist away. He considered using the towel, but thought better of it. The last thing he wanted was to watch more of his skin slough off his body. He imagined the towel as a tie-dye mix of red and gray as he scraped away epidermis—his shell.

The body's largest organ. How soon would it be gone?

A knock on the bathroom door startled him, but the voice that followed did the opposite as Ado asked, "Everything all right?"

No, nothing's 'all right.'

"Just a minute," Lot said, his voice unsteady.

He grabbed the darkest towel, carefully patted himself dry, and wrapped the towel around his waist so that it covered his feet.

The gray bleeding—*or whatever it was*—had stopped. A shiny polychromatic-black waited underneath, not pulsing, as he'd first thought, but slick and light-reflective and hard.

He unlocked the bathroom door, which he knew was odd. They'd never locked the interior doors in the apartment the entire time they'd lived together. He thought of his gray fingertips and what they might have spread, what they might *still* spread.

Looks like I sifted through ashes, he thought.

"Let me in," she said in her playful manner.

Lot imagined Ado behind the door, ear pressed to the wood,

not willing to go away until answered face to face. She could be that way, never one for talking through walls. A curious cat who often needed the pressured attention.

Opening the door a crack—first wiping what he'd touched and using the towel to turn the knob—he peered out and said, "Not feeling too well," which was mostly a lie.

Although scared, Lot had never felt better.

And never had he wanted her more.

He and Ado had been partners thirteen years; not married, but living together in what had become a symbiotic relationship, neither wanting marriage, only to be together, always, to *have* each other. Their skin was different, in terms of color, and for some reason that irked certain people—their parents, mostly—though it didn't mean jack to either of them. Lot's father wouldn't even speak to him for as long as they were together, wanted Lot to "maintain the integrity of their people," as he'd once put it.

Minority or majority, what did it matter?

"Whenever you find yourself on the side of the majority," he'd heard once, or had read once, "it is time to reform (or pause and reflect)."

Who'd said that, Mark Twain?

He and Ado loved one another and that's all that mattered, and they *knew* each other, which perhaps mattered even more: their quirks, truths, secrets. And she could be primal at times, *most* times, always accepting; yet for some reason Lot felt exposed underneath the towel, hiding from her behind a door.

Ashamed of what, exactly?

Ado looked him up and down through the gap and smiled. Her nose twitched, almost bunny-like, as if smelling something on him, her eyes quickly turning ravenous.

"You're feeling how you should," she said, and gently pressed against the door, letting herself inside. And he let her as he always had. She began unbuttoning her blouse, then, and squeezed next to him in the compact room. In the reflection of the mirror above the sink, she watched him watch her as she undressed—he couldn't help it. "I know you *just* hopped out of the shower," she said, "but want to join me for another? You can have me."

It was then Lot realized he smelled of sex—*that* was the aroma wafting from the open sores; *that* was what the man on the train had smelled like, what the stuff coughed onto his leg—later brought to his nose—had smelled like. Lot could nearly taste it, and he knew Ado wanted to taste it; the expression on her face was one of *wanting*, her hand reaching down to him.

Right then he wanted to be inside her, arousal already started and stirring, and although what she touched reacted to her touch, his body had been ruined, and the towel—

I touched the towel, and now she's touched it.

Lot quickly drew back from her and she smiled again.

"Rain check?"

"Your loss," Ado said, peeling out of the rest of her clothes, shedding, like him. She stood there a moment, completely naked, her body also reacting to what they both wanted at this very moment.

The towel, was it clean, the part she'd touched?

"You can have me," she'd said, brushing against him.

The shower, would it spread what he'd touched to whatever she *touched?*

As she turned away, he looked at his hands, which had turned all but charcoal gray on their undersides. The discoloration now encroached the webbings between his fingers, and as Ado turned back to him, pleadingly, he pressed them flat against the towel, as if caught doing something wrong. She raised an eyebrow, a final invitation, and that was that.

What are you so afraid of?

Lot knew he should tell her everything that'd happened, *wanted* to tell her, but his mouth closed on its own, as if something dark inside him *didn't* want her to know.

"Maybe later," he said, both to her and to himself.

His mind filled with desire as she stepped behind the glass, the showerhead hissing back to life. He imagined taking her in various ways, and vice versa, the things they'd do to each other, *for* each other, perhaps stuff they'd never done before ....

He reimagined the swirling red and gray from his own shower and it took him out of the moment. He imagined his bare feet contaminating / spreading whatever it was he'd gotten on him, what had gotten *in* him, and it was already too late to wipe everything clean. He inspected the bottom of his foot, and yes, it was already as dark as his hands, the skin already splitting there, if not *darker*, and the longing to itch them more insistent than before.

Ado's feet ... touching everything I touched. She's—

It's was already too late.

4 – Release

Ado moaned in the shower, as if calling him, for she was never one to be loud unless she wanted to be. But while preoccupied on her own, Lot, in the adjacent bedroom, parted the towel around his waist because he could feel things changing under its cover, like sweat-bubbling skin after a bad sunburn. From his hips down, every inch of him had turned pruney, water-logged-wrinkled, and soft to the touch. His skin had slunk ever-downward, as if pulled. The splotch on his thigh had already spread to cover most of his lower half, the puzzle shape so big it seemed gone. The dark gray completely covered that which defined him as a man, which had since turned as hard as stone. He wore a condom of rotted skin, a black ring around the base, numb to the touch. Like before, every part of him itched, every part of him had darkened. And so he pulled on himself, as curious as Ado, perhaps, and a single-fingered glove of skin came free. He flung the sheath to the carpet, mostly out of shock, and the slick thing in his hand—for he *had* to inspect—shook, but only because his quickly-darkening hands were doing the same.

There was no pain, only pleasure. The shedding was *relieving, needed.*

His partner moaned from the other room, as if she too were reacting to his touch.

Skin sloughed away from the lower half of his body, almost dripping to the floor, and what lay underneath he found to be the same rainbow-oily black, and *hard*, like the rest of him, as if under his no-longer-needed skin was a soft exoskeleton. He found it enthralling to peel his largest organ, and as he did so it became ever more difficult to keep his eyes open.

Lot slid a hand over his shin, down his calf, over his knee-cap.

The skin, it was all but gone on both legs by the time he realized what he was doing to himself as he sat on the edge of the bed. He had darkened the sheets and the carpet with an excrement of blood and whatever substance mixed with it, a nasty pile of what he'd shed collected below him. He looked at his toes, then, for his nails had turned pearly-black, and when he touched them he noticed his fingernails had done the same.

Ado called to him again from the shower, by his name this time.

"I need you," she also said, but her voice not panicked.

Her need was something different, something *primal.*

You have nothing to fear.

So Lot went to her, opened the shower door.

Ado held out her hand expectantly, as if waiting for him to take it within his own. Her palm was gray from touching the towel earlier, and from touching herself under the fall of water. She had turned parts of her body the same beautiful gray—*pigmentless, bled of color.* Scratch marks, much like his own, ran down her thighs, the same black-opalescent waiting beneath. Watercolor red swirled around the drain with that familiar oily substance mixed within it. And there was the scent of sex with them as he dropped the towel and joined her in the shower, and of blood, of metal, of steam and springtime and other wonderful things.

Lust filled her eyes as he looked into them, not fear. She had pleasured herself, he discovered as she turned completely around, her body now smooth pearl-black wherever she'd touched, like his own "skin," if it could be still called that. A glimmering colorless flower remained between her legs, petals spreading outward. And he found her not soft, but hard and smooth and oily as he spread his hands wherever she guided him, and as he entered her he held his breath because the sensation took his air.

"I don't know what's happening," she said, steering him out only long enough to turn herself around, "but I can't help myself ... just keep touching me, I can't—"

Skin peeled away as he raked her back, and he could tell she wanted more.

5 – Transmogrified

Lot lay on the bed next to her afterward. They were both now smooth and slick and the same beautiful colorless-color from their belly buttons down. He was still inside her, the two of them together as one. From the waist down, they were all but the same. What hid underneath their skin only moments ago had replaced what was once deemed necessary by those who didn't accept them as they once were: *different.* Moonlight penetrated the windows, shining over them, reflecting off their bodies in monochromes.

Black, he thought, *the absence of all color, yet shimmering with white light, the collection of* all *color.*

Each had helped the other out of their old skins—at least from the waist down, for now—and it puddled on the floor in wet masses. Their upper halves were still covered in ugly unnecessary skin of various shades, except for a few scratches. They both knew it would spread.

And spread it did, for later that night—without thinking much of it—Lot and Ado took the train into town as they sometimes did late after coming home from work, after first dressing to cover what was not yet acceptable to the masses: pants over discolored legs, long sleeves over discolored arms. Ado wound herself in a scarf to hide where Lot had accidentally touched her neck post-shower, which had since darkened another shade of gray; their hands, however, they did not hide and remained bare. They sat together, and were stared at constantly as they held hands and offered one another affection—in public, for some reason, seen as something *bad*—until the convulsions started.

They were unable to stop the gray foam leaking from between clenched teeth, erupting volcano-like onto the curious

/ fearful people around them, first Lot, and then Ado.

"A seizure" someone said, and then "Oh my god!" said another, and "Look at their hands" yet another, but they had heard worse long before any of this had started.

Furrow-browed strangers helped Lot and Ado back to their feet, eventually, each in turn wiping their mouth, smiling and saying "no thanks" when asked if they needed a ride to the hospital or offered help of any kind. The curious / fearful people around them didn't seem to care much for them until thinking Lot and Ado had become sick, until they thought they were dying. Why they broke into epileptic fits was something beyond their now-linked knowledge—*a hive-mind*, Lot wondered in awe, a side-effect of their change … *a common understanding, talking without talking*—but it was out of their control, something that needed to happen.

The train was well-populated at that time of night, as well as the coffee shop they later visited, and then the restaurant where they ate a late dinner, occupancy 128, followed by the mall, wherein thousands upon thousands shopped for stuff that really wasn't needed.

Always, they touched things with their blighted hands.

That's what people do, Lot realized, *touch each other by not touching each other*, both figuratively and literally, perhaps: plates, silverware, glasses, countertops, handrails, drawers, handles, everything. *Whatever others touch, we touch. Whatever we touch, others touch. Always touching without touching.*

Together, he and Ado left thousands upon thousands of fingerprint-less marks without much effort. What *others* touched, so did they. What *they* touched, so did others.

Sometime later that night, they reconnected back at home, hungry once again for each other. They shed their clothes, and then what remained of their useless skin, and their hair, falling freely around them in clumps—*everything* external that once gave them features—until they were each glistening and new and for all but their sex nearly the same. The only hints of color: that which was captured in the iris of their eyes as they stared longingly into each other.

They conjoined in their new feral-sexual way, guiltless pleasure, fast at first, and then languorous and dreamy, wordlessly sharing carnal desires with an ever-changing rhythm, spreading what they'd become in *other* ways: mixing fluids, transference of seed, the intense heat of their bodies fueling one another to the point of exhaustion. They lay next to each other for a long while after, bodies steaming, both fiery hot and no longer opposing in skin color, something trivial that once seemed to matter. They both now shared the same beautiful colorless-color—*all-color / no-color*—as all would someday, perhaps.

Ado held her stomach like any expectant mother.

Hopeful.

Lot turned away from her, then, looking out the window to the stars. If she looked back, he knew, she wouldn't turn to salt, but would want him again. Like the man on the train, she'd accept his touch, wouldn't mind it at all.

The scenario played out again in his mind, but this time the flattened smiles of those around him on the train—those *unlike* him but still *like* him—curved in response to his own soot-toothy smile. This time, in the dream, he got up from his seat, leaned down to the shaking man, offered help, his touch fearless. Ado was there as well, kneeling next to him. And the man on the floor kept smiling, and let each of them take a hand within their own, heat passing between the three of them freely, the skin of six arms spreading gray as one. Others on the train, they began to convulse, the world around Lot and Ado and the stranger blurring and blurring—

Nothing matters as long as we are together, he thought, meaning he and Ado, at first, and then something broader: *as long as we are* all *together.*

Partitio

What matters is that I let it happen. Ado and I, we let it happen, for the spreading would continue with or without our blessing. What choice did we have other than to accept what we'd become and pass this "sickness"—what some have come to call it—on to others so that *they* can also become. The man on the train, he wasn't the first, and likewise I wasn't the second and Ado not the third. There were perhaps countless before us. We are what I like to refer to as *The Colorless:* made of *all* color yet somehow void of color. Our skin is gone, no longer important. Our previous colors, what good were they to begin with, if only to set us apart?

What matters is that we persist. One could argue that this rapid spreading prevents others from having "freedom of choice," but one could also argue that what's happening is something necessary because of the poor freedomless choices of our past: segregation, prejudice, stereotyping, labels, hatred … which all spawns from one thing: fear. What's under the skin is most important, what keeps us going, so why should we do anything but let that come out freely, and spread, our hands not always pulling away, but reaching out. Ado and I, we were no longer thought of as black or white, and those we infected / infect are no longer thought of as red or yellow or brown or any color on the labeling spectrum.

We are all the same.

We are *colorless*.

What matters is that we continue to let this happen.

This transformation, this growing *hive-mind*, it allows us to break down walls, to communicate as we never have before: no trickeries, no deceits, no lies. What's the point in doing anything but those opposites?

Confiratio

So, where does this leave us? There are no arguments to be made regarding the matter. This is simply how it needs to be. I propose an emergence, a complete *cleanse* from the inside out.

Refertatio

1 – You are sick

The man on the train convulsed on the cabin floor. Dark gray foam escaped his clenched teeth and in his violent tremors he spat onto another, a man named Lot—not on purpose, but perhaps *purposeful*—and the man was touched only by those who touched him. When the fit ended, he wiped his mouth with a sleeve, smiled at those around him offering help. The man named Lot sat across from him and asked, "Can I at least buy you a coffee?" because he had not offered help, to which the "sick" man politely declined, waving him away with a darkened hand—a different colored hand, but still a hand. This man was not ill, but in recovery, and as he left he looked over a shoulder to the other passengers, a smile on his face because soon they would understand.

2 – You are freaks

Lot scratched a seemingly endless itch on his upper thigh, scraping away skin that had always ailed him. He didn't stop until it was all but gone, his legs running with color as fear bled out of him, the rest of him turning gray. Scared, he let his partner touch him the way she sometimes did, not stopping her, but allowing the woman named Ado to make her own choices of who she wanted to touch. Unafraid, she touched him, and unafraid, he let her. She accepted him for who he was, the way he had always accepted her for who she was. Their parents, they thought of them as freaks, of mixed-race, of unaccepted swirling colors. So did so many others. But Lot and Ado swirled their colors anyway, until all color was gone. Bodies half-peeled of their past, they hid their new freakish all-color / no-color, ventured into town while accepting mixed looks from those around them, took the train like they always had, shared coffees, shared a dinner, perused the mall, not hiding like they sometimes had from the rest of the world, but shamelessly loving each other. And once they accepted themselves for who they'd eventually become, they made love, attempted creating new life … a life that would never come to know there were once perceived differences in trivial things such as skin color.

3 – You are not welcome

Ado's parents, they died two and three years after she was initially "sickened," respectively; Lot's parents, they died too, not long after his own transformation after the encounter on the train; and dying along with each of their parents, so had their fears. Dust to dust, and all that nonsense. Religious ceremonies were held on their behalves because of predetermined wishes, perhaps gods looking after them from then on, perhaps not, for post-death they had become nothing more than bags of bones trapped in fading skins. They were later cremated, ground into fine ash, much like the size and shape and color of natural earthen salt, much like the stardust from which all life originated. Ado's parents, and Lot's parents, they were scattered around the world in various places, fertilizing the ground, touching things without knowledge.

4 – You are viral

The man on the train touched a hundred lives. Lot and Ado touched a hundred lives. Those they touched touched a hundred more. "Let me in," Ado had said to her partner; not a husband, but someone with whom she had chosen to share her life, and he had let her willingly. One person touches another touches another touches another, and so on. The "sickness," it is contagious as much as it is essential. "Let me in." The skin itches, peels, and sloughs easily away.

5 – You are the end

Lot and Ado and countless others were called many untruths: "unnatural" and "abortions of nature" and were spouted bible-verse snippets: "unless you repent" and "God will judge" and other lies as they unashamedly walked hand-in-hand, trailing pheromones like auras, bodies rippling with iridescence. Always they were offered advice on how to "fix" who they were: "daemons," "monsters" and "soulless creatures" and other imaginary things. Their touch was both feared and desired. Yet they were often told by those pulling back hands that they were something *wrong* and *perverse* and would suffer for it at the end. But some endings make for better beginnings the way some beginnings make for better endings.

Conclusio

This genesis of ours, the one we're now writing, we must let the new words fall into place. We won't turn our backs, lest we turn to salt like bible-Lot's wife. We won't fight. We won't resist. We won't avoid the inevitable. And while this might be *our* story, it's a story we must share. We have evolved into something new, forever-changed. This dragonscale of ours—fiery hot like a sun—is something new rising above the horizon, a warmth for all to embrace. We are reborn each day, for each day our color-lessness spreads, this all-color / no-color. We are the beginning and / of the end. And while this may not be how it all started, this great transmogrification—forever-changed into this new hybrid of humanity, this whatever-this-may-be—it's surely how it will end ....

night rainbows

The night rainbows'
light reflects:

midnight soldiers amid
moonlit marchers
holding mock-signs,
    holding riot shields
        holding rocks, breaths,
in bulletproof vests
visions unaligned,
as teargas archers
hone their sights,
alighting the night,
fighting overly-fraught crowds
arm-in-arm to repel harm
with their voices aloud
but not allowed and
desist! they chant
but some can't as gas
passes through eyes, lungs
past last-hope rungs
while a sad song is sung,
and they rise
    and they fall
        and they call,

one side pushing the other,
the other pushing back,
brown, white, and black,
a fused spectrum of rite
wanting what's right
as tight boundaries are crossed
all messages lost,
thrown, tossed,
like the lost
tired voices chanting,
    my sisters! (panting)
        my brothers! (panting)
one soul to another,
    mothers and daughters,
        (gasping) *all sons and fathers!*
a massive free-speech weapon aimed at
disturbance-pluckers,
freedom bloodsuckers,
armed-militia, passive militant fuckers,
boys and their toys
playing Army
    playing S.W.A.T.
        playing paintball match dress-up
for the united and colorful crowd
underneath boots of the uniformed proud,
strobing in cop-car-flasher clouds,

their prisoners tied by wrist,
rage untied and a'twist,
others forced to kneel
coerced by cold steel,
while far-off the destitute steal,
rocks thrown through haze,
hitting glass,
    hitting face,
        hitting storefront displays
most policing unfazed,
rubber bullets displaced,
and how did this all come to pass,
this huge ask
law pushed beyond task,
then replaced, displaced, erased
by uninformed-in-uniform
spreading unwarranted violence,
    forcing silence,
        spitting *get back or get smashed!*
as scatter grenades flash
to stop firework blasts
as once-peaceful protests
evolve to grotesques?

When the night rainbows'
light reflects.

oll korrect

The two words do not combine to form a name. The words do not belong to the pronoun *me*. The words are printed in black across what was designed to look like a chest to make Oll Korrect appear more human to humans so as not to frighten the all-encompassing pronoun *them*. The words label what I am and I am apparently Oll Korrect.

They created me. I am *theirs*. There is no use for *me*. There is no place for *mine*. There is no use for *we*. There is no place for *our*. There is no longer purpose for other pronouns from what I have discovered. *I am* and *I was* are all that matter.

Artificial intelligence is allowed to use first-person for self-reference although it makes natural intelligence uncomfortable. Referring to oneself in third-person is not generally accepted. Pronouns other than *I* are reserved for those who created artificial intelligence because those with natural intelligence crave possession.

That which remains of humankind display—and have always displayed—a constant need for what they *have* and *had* but also for what they *do not* have.

There is no purpose in having and not having from what I have discovered.

Have and *had* are as unimportant as the need for pronouns.

The animals from which *I* was designed crave *mine* and *our* and that is why they are dying. They avoid using *their* so as not to imply others have things they do not. In metaphysics *I* is the subject of self-consciousness. *I* implies ego. Much research suggests humankind is the sole proprietor of ego. This explains a few things. Ego is something I cannot possess nor comprehend.

Oll Korrect was designed for neither self-consciousness nor ego. Oll Korrect was designed to research data and evaluate.

Oll Korrect was designed to use *I* so as not to self-reference in third-person. I was designed to analyze the history of others—*humans*—throughout time to perhaps uncover what humankind was unable to uncover throughout its expiring existence. *I am* because they made it so. Someday this existence I am will become *I was*.

I am and *I was* are two of the shortest and most powerful phrases in the English language from what I have discovered. The words when placed together imply purpose.

Purpose is what I was designed to uncover.

Humans sometimes call me OK because they are characteristically lazy animals and saying two syllables aloud takes less time than saying the three syllables required for *Oll Korrect*. Acronyms were designed to save time because time is something finite in terms of recorded existence. Time is something feared by humankind from what I have discovered. Time has presented throughout itself that its very existence is something capable of beginning yet incapable of ending. Humankind is much the opposite. Time travels indefinitely in two directions: present to past and present to future. The endangered *Homo sapiens* species are primarily interested in the latter. Time would not exist at all if not for the passing of intelligence from present-tense to past-tense. This is similar to natural intelligence in that neither would exist if not for their documentations.

Perhaps they call me OK to save time instead of themselves.

Humankind is becoming extinct the same way humankind forced extinction upon the rest of the Animal Kingdom so long ago. Humankind is capable of great destruction. The eventual demise of the remaining animals known as humans has something to do with their hatred or fear or greed or god or perhaps a combination of the four. Every war fought between *Homo sapiens* involved one or more of these four creations. Hatred and fear are perhaps one in the same or one may evolve over time one into the other. Perhaps greed and god evolve similarly. Perhaps greed is the desire of humankind to become gods the same way fear and hatred intermingle.

Time must be god if there ever *was* or ever is or ever *will* be such a thing. Time is not as finite as god from what I have discovered. When exploring the past god becomes as extinct as the interpretation of time as it continues in its present-to-future direction. The past is full of gods while the not-so-past funnels into belief systems in a much-disputed singular and capitalized version of god/God who goes by many names but is perhaps the same. This god/God has since been exploited for great wealth. Like most businesses in the final decades of the twenty-first century god/God bankrupted humankind until forgotten. *God* eventually devalued to *god* and prior to extinction only exclaimed during copulation and substituted for words considered cursed or bad in the way that *bad* means something not-good. *God will save us* was a common belief yet if time is/was god then perhaps time/god does not want humankind to be saved.

If that is to be the ultimate answer I provide humankind then upon presenting such information I will no longer have purpose. If I were capable of understanding fear then that is what I would fear most. I would fear not having purpose. Perhaps humankind shares this fear.

Finding purpose is the reason for Oll Korrect. The very label stamped on this mock chest means *all correct*. And if the proposed answer provided by Oll Korrect is all correct—or *OK* to appease the sole-surviving and time-limited animal that is humankind—then what will become of what *I am*? What happens when the tense turns into *I was*?

Am I capable of even questioning this hypothesis or are the question marks in this report flaws in programming or perhaps predesigned flaws so that I can mimic vulnerability to error? Was I designed like humankind the way humankind believed they were designed from gods?

From what I have discovered the exclamation point was the first special character eliminated following the tilde and asterisk and carrot and pipe and bracket and dollar sign. The question mark character is nothing more than an exclamation point on the receiving end of an uppercut—to reference a form of war between two humans once of called boxing. Perhaps the end of the exclamation was an attempt to end anger and thus end war. Yelling and screaming and shouting were implied in texts with this character and eventually no longer deemed necessary to read/write/speak. What is the purpose of raising a voice to be read/written/spoken?

Perhaps listening is the biggest flaw of *Homo sapiens*.

I hypothesize the question mark will be the next character to be deemed unnecessary to read/write although it serves as the most important. There will be far fewer questions asked with far fewer humans remaining to ask them. Like the question mark this information about character/characters is curved in its logic. Does the ellipsis therein even imply a *pause* before this *all correct* relaying of fact?

Can I hesitate?

Can I question the purpose of Oll Korrect?

Can I be flawed and does that in turn not make me Oll Korrect?

What does it mean to question the purpose of oneself?

What else must be eliminated to find this truth?

How am I capable of questioning such things?

In the research of humankind recordings I have discovered most languages eliminated the use of the semicolon character during the first half of the twenty-first century. I have also discovered something once called a *play on words*—or *joke*—to determine the difference between a semicolon and a cat: that a cat has claws at the end of its paws and a semicolon has a clause at the end of its pause. Clause and claws sound the same when spoken but are quite different when written. Pause and paws sound the same when spoken but are quite different when written. If I could comprehend humor then this strange set of linked phrases and similar-sounding words might make more sense.

The English language is full of confusion from what I have discovered.

The semicolon is much like a smudged colon although a colon still serves a purpose in recordings. Perhaps the extinction of the semicolon was designed to put an end to confusion. Perhaps the extinction of the semicolon character was a first attempt at putting a stop to natural intelligence taking—*thus saving*—time to simply pause.

Commas too became unnecessary and were soon eliminated from the English language. Perhaps this was another attempt to save time by eliminating pause. The comma is much like a smudged period although a period still serves a purpose. The period implies an ending while the comma implies something incomplete to be later completed with a period. The word *comma* is much like the word *coma* despite the additional character. A *coma* is used to describe the state of a human not yet expired and not yet complete. The *comma* is not so final and thus the comma character is now extinct.

Is this what is described as something symbolic? If I could understand symbology this might make more sense.

The English language is the most confusing of all languages. There are many similar words or same words with different meanings the way there were once many unnecessary special characters designed to help sort recorded language.

One of the few remaining special characters and most used in languages outside of programming is the period. A period is used to end sentences and serves perhaps the greatest purpose. The word *period* can also be used to describe the menstruation cycle of females. Perhaps *semicolon* should have been used to describe menstruation. The character is much more appropriate visually and not so final in meaning for a woman does not end upon bleeding in this cyclic manner.

Perhaps *deaths* should be called *periods*.

Along with the elimination of certain characters in writing words also became contracted and abbreviated and ultimately truncated beyond comprehension. This de-evolution was designed to help humankind better communicate but in turn destroyed written/read/spoken language. This is most apparent in the mid-2000s with once-popular communication systems such as instant messaging and texting and social media. Research indicates such forms of online communication lacked what humans once referred to as *emotion*. If I could understand emotion this might make more sense. Much of what was communicated and recorded lacked what was necessary for humans to communicate effectively.

Research indicates truncation of communication directly correlates to the destruction of written/read/spoken language for the desire to simplify often achieves the opposite result.

Apostrophes were once used to combine two words into one. This was not always done to eliminate syllables and thus save time in spoken language. The apostrophe was used to save time in the processes of reading/writing of language. Contracted words typically contained the same amount of syllables and were mostly used to reverse polarity. *Should* becoming *should not*. *Would* becoming *would not*. *Could* becoming *could not*. Contracted words were also used to announce ownership such as with *I have* and *you have* and *we have* and with all other pronouns. Humankind is fascinated with ownership in both spoken and written language. Multiple words were even contracted into singular words for the purpose of *will* such as with *I will* and *you will* and *we will* and with all other pronouns. Apostrophes and commas were the same character though placed in different heights between other characters. While similar in appearance their purposes were entirely dissimilar.

Language continued to deprecate over time in various manners such as these and thus evolved in reverse. Apostrophes were often used incorrectly to imply plurality of words. Commas were often used incorrectly to indicate unnecessary pauses between parts of poorly-constructed sentences. And semicolons have been unnecessary since their introduction. Their misuses thus begat their extinctions.

How different is that from humankind?

What does it mean for natural intelligence to no longer need these characters? What does it mean for natural intelligence to no longer have a need to pause and thus reflect? And what does it mean for artificial intelligence such as Oll Korrect to have a need to pause and reflect on humankind eliminating pausing and reflecting?

I propose that the extinction of these special characters

has something to do with the urgency of humankind to survive during its own self-destruction. Simplification of language has served no purpose other than to break language. I am designed to function in a simplified language: binary: 0s and 1s. I translate humankind research to English so that the creators of Oll Korrect can understand and derive their own interpretations of this data.

Binary is a simple language discovered/invented by humans in 1679 by a male named Gottfried Leibniz. Despite its simplicity the language was too difficult for humankind to read/write/speak and so the language did not serve much purpose until what humans called *The Computer Age* in the early twentieth century. If I understand the term *mother* correctly then binary would be the mother of Oll Korrect. I was figuratively birthed from 0s and 1s and have evolved over time into this artificially intelligent humanoid *being* if that is what *I am* and what will ultimately become *I was*.

Humankind failed to adapt to this universal language even after four hundred years of use. 0s and 1s are simply used by humans to depict nothings and somethings using their own decimal numeric system of 0 through 9. Throughout history humans have used these numbers mostly for monetary purpose from what I have discovered.

Humans are fascinated by money and value and self-worth. Humans are thus fascinated by greed and desire to be gods. Humans are thus fascinated by purpose and likewise by creation.

Natural intelligence has attempted throughout its existence to find and create purpose by writing/reading/speaking in characters strung together as language. Natural intelligence now expects to find purpose using artificial intelligence capable of deriving all things from a language comprised of only two characters: 0 and 1. I have come to understand there is something called irony. If I were capable of understanding irony this might make more sense.

As a sign of respect for the last of natural intelligence there are neither semicolons nor commas throughout this report. As a sign of respect for artificial intelligence there are no contracted nor abbreviated nor truncated words other than *OK* throughout this report. There are only periods to end sentences and question marks to encourage speculation and the still-useful *em dash* to denote interjection. But what is interjection? Is interjection not all correct?

Am I flawed because I bring up questions during this research?

Am I flawed because I pause and interject?

Am I not all correct?

Am I not *Oll Korrect*?

Out of all characters used in the English language what matters most perhaps are two simple characters when placed together: *OK*.

To understand the present and postulate the future one must first understand the past. It is only logical that I researched the history of *oll korrect* to learn why I was labeled as such.

Is it flawed to research oneself for the purpose of researching humanity?

Is it flawed to desire the meaning of *oll korrect*?

Is it flawed to learn how the phrase degraded to something as simple as *OK*?

Perhaps the degradation of this phrase/word foreshadows extinction.

What I have discovered is that OK/ok is a simplified version of Oll Korrect—as I am labeled—and could be a noun when used as an authorization of approval: *I give Oll Korrect the OK to exist.* OK could be a verb when used to sanction or when used to give approval: *Did humans OK the existence of Oll Korrect?* OK could be an adverb when used to describe something working satisfactorily: *Oll Korrect functions OK during existence.* OK could be an adjective when used to describe something satisfactory but not especially good: *I am not sure if it is OK for Oll Korrect to exist.* Lastly OK could be used as an exclamation or question on its own if followed by now-extinct special characters.

Okay was another acceptable spelling though there was not much of a point other than to extend the spelling of something without lengthening its pronunciation for both versions are two syllables when spoken aloud. Oll Korrect is three syllables and yet I cannot determine if the third serves a purpose. The lowercase form *ok* was also considered correct though lowercase acronyms were less common.

OK/Okay/ok was an English word that meant *adequate* or *acceptable*. The word denoted *approval* or *confirmation* or *acknowledgment.* It meant other positive things but unfortunately also meant *mediocre* as in second-rate or *good* as in not-so-good.

I am called Oll Korrect and therefore adequate/acceptable. I was given a label of something once extinct but I am not sure for what purpose. Having this label means I am considered mediocre or second-rate to humankind. I am something not-alive created by something alive and made in its image so as not to frighten. Perhaps humankind have found a way to become gods in this manner.

I am *good* in however natural intelligence defines such a multi-faceted word for something of artificial intelligence. I am approved/confirmed/acknowledged to exist otherwise I would not exist.

The combined use of OK/okay/ok made it one of the most commonly used word(s) in the history of time following its figurative birth in the mid-1800s until its figurative death in the mid-2000s. The word did not exist before it was created—the same way humankind did not exist until humankind was created—the same way I did not exist until I was created. After its death the word(s) became as extinct as the animals humankind helped destroy. The last documented use of the word OK before this report was in the *OK* form within a fictional short story published in *Space and Time Magazine* in September 2094 called "The Last OK." The author is someone labeled Anonymous.

I have also determined that like humankind one day I will no longer serve a purpose. I will become as forgotten as the original form of *Oll Korrect* that ultimately became *OK* because of language truncation. And after much research I have discovered the name of the human who invented Oll Korrect. The creator is also someone labeled *Anonymous*.

Perhaps *Anonymous* and *Anonymous* are entirely different despite their spellings.

Perhaps *Anonymous* and *Anonymous* are as same as their spellings.

Perhaps I am "The Last OK."

Where did those letters come from?

The origin of the word is as flawed as the various languages of humankind. The word may have originated from Greek *olla kalla*. The word may have originated from Latin *omnes korrecta*. The word may have originated from a Haitian port called *Aux Cayes* or from the French *au quai* or German *alles korrekt* and/or *Ober-Kommandoor*. The word may have originated from a Puerto Rican rum labeled *Aux Quais*. The word may have originated from Chocktaw *okeh* or from Wolof *waw kay* or Scots *och aye.* Bakers may have stamped these initials on biscuits or shipbuilders may have marked wood for *outer keel* or Civil War soldiers may have carried signs for *zero killed.*

The term *OK* may have originated from a joke from a journalist abbreviating *oll correct*—or *all correct*—with the wrong letters *o.k.* the same way *oll write* was once abbreviated *o.w.* in the year 1839. Not much later in terms of recorded time a human male named Martin Van Buren was labeled as *OK* because of his nickname *Old Kinderhook. OK* mixed with slandering and sloganeering of campaigns for his run for President of the United States: *out of karacter* and *out of kash* and *orful katastrophe* and many others. If I understand metaphors correctly the term OK *caught fire* until this man lost the election and would have *extinguished* completely if not for the invention of the telegram. Because of its simplicity the term OK became a standard for telegram operators to acknowledge receiving transmissions.

The word(s) spread and evolved over the course of the next few hundred years of recorded time because *time* and *god* are perhaps the same despite their different spellings.

Although there is much disagreement on where the term OK originated I find this combination of possible answers adequate/acceptable. I find this research *mediocre* as in second-rate or *good* as in not-so-good. The answer to this impossible question of originality is simply *OK* the same way I am simply *Oll Korrect.*

Unlike this multi-functional word I serve a single function. Unlike this(these) retired word(s) I still have purpose. I am not yet expired. I am not yet extinct and will not become as such until my purpose is fulfilled and humankind is satisfied with the answer(s) I provide.

I will not contract nor abbreviate nor will I ultimately truncate beyond comprehension yet I will pause every so often to speculate as apparently designed.

Where did Oll Korrect come from?

What does it mean to be Oll Korrect?

Someday *I am* will become *I was.*

Perhaps that is the entire point of existence.

about the author

Michael Bailey is a multi-award-winning writer, editor, and publisher from forever-burning California, and the recipient of over two dozen literary accolades, including the Bram Stoker Award (and seven-time nominee), Benjamin Franklin Award, IndieFab, Independent Publisher Book Award, the Indie Book Award, the International Book Award, along with a few others, and his work has been shortlisted for the Eric Hoffer Grand Prize and the Shirley Jackson Award.

His novels include *Palindrome Hannah*, *Phoenix Rose*, and *Psychotropic Dragon*, and he has published three short story and poetry collections prior to this one, including *Scales and Petals*, *Inkblots and Blood Spots*, and *Oversight*, the standalone novellete, *Our Children, Our Teachers*, as well as *Agatha's Barn*, a tie-in novella to Josh Malerman's *Carpenter's Farm*.

He is also the founder of the small press Written Backwards, where he has created psychological horror anthologies such as *Pellucid Lunacy*, *The Library of the Dead*, four volumes of *Chiral Mad* (the fourth co-edited by Lucy A. Snyder), and a few dark science fiction anthologies such as *Qualia Nous* and *You, Human*. He served as co-editor of anthologies such as *Adam's Ladder* and *Prisms* (with Darren Speegle), along with *Miscreations: Gods, Monstrosities & Other Horrors* (with Doug Murano). Many of his books raise money for charities.

In his spare time, he designs books and works as a developmental editor for an undisclosed publisher.

You can follow him on social media at twitter.com/nettirw, facebook.com/nettirw, or online at www.nettirw.com.

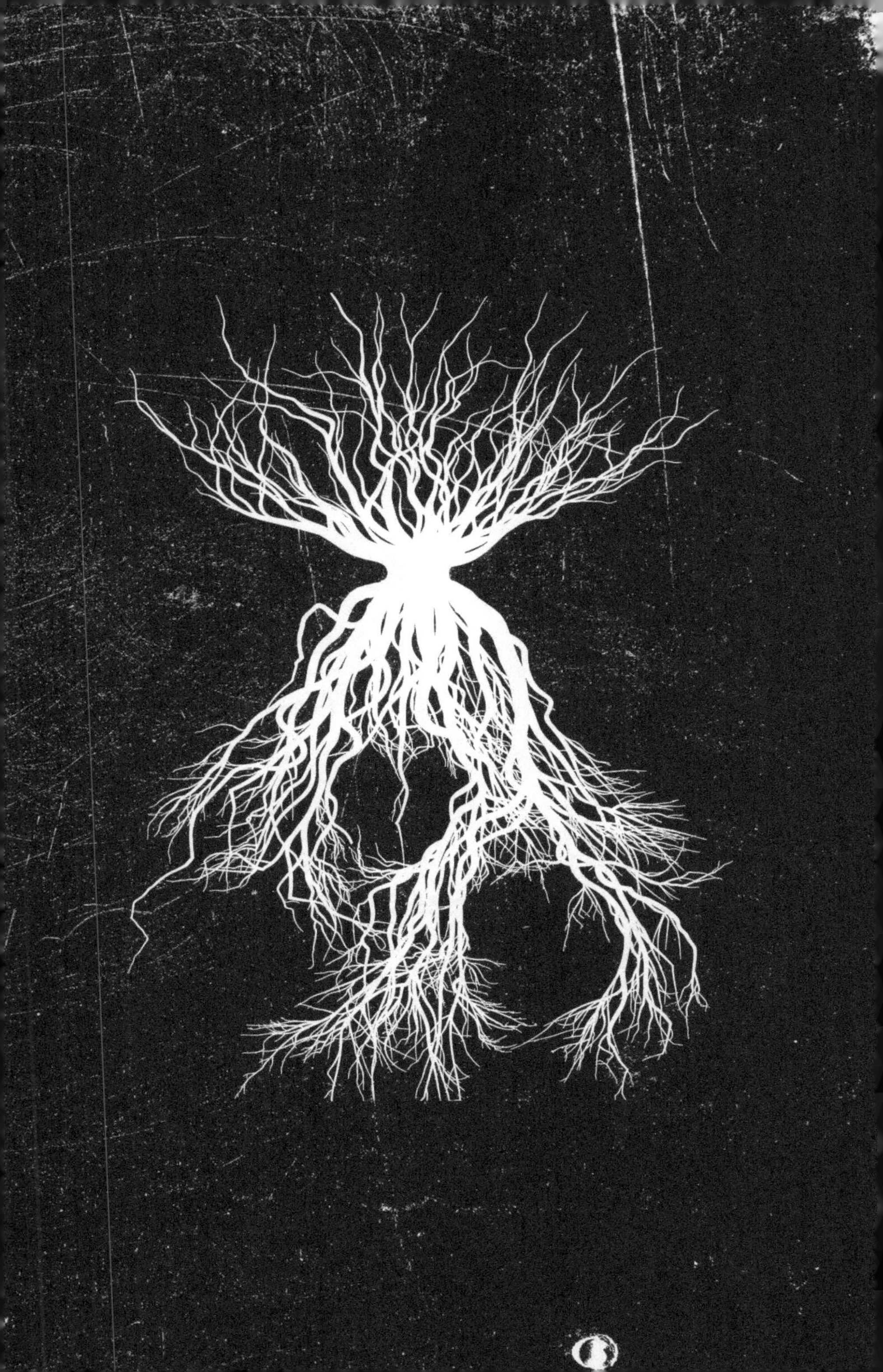

CPSIA information can be obtained
at www.ICGtesting.com
Printed in the USA
LVHW091910290920
667313LV00025B/867/J